A Reluct.

By
John Pilkington

© John Pilkington 2023.

John Pilkington has asserted his rights under the Copyright, Design and Patents Act, 1988, to be identified as the author of this work.

First published in 2023 by Sharpe Books.

'There are more than two hundred men of all ages who, at the instigation of the Jesuits, conspire to kill me.'
(Queen Elizabeth 1st, letter to the French Ambassador Michel de Castelnau)

A RELUCTANT HERO

ONE

It was supposed to be one last mission, but Will Revill didn't believe it.

Why would he? After two years of being forced to carry out dangerous assignments for England's Vice-Chamberlain and spymaster Sir Thomas Heneage, and having long since decided that Heneage was one of the most unscrupulous men he had ever met, his expectations were at rock-bottom. He said as much to his lover Jenna, as they sat outside their cottage in the golden light of a summer sunset.

'Yet, you knew it couldn't last,' Jenna said.

'What couldn't last?' He enquired, feeling a yawn coming on. It had been a long day on the farm, and he was weary.

'Hiding away down here.'

'Hiding?' He threw her a wry look. 'And there was I thinking this was what you wanted.'

'A quiet life, yes.' She looked out across the meadow where cows grazed, towards a distant treeline that marked the border of Petrus Burwood's land. 'But we're not free – or at least, you aren't. Sooner or later, Heneage was going to call you to London.'

Revill made no reply. He knew she was right, as he knew that Heneage, who had eyes everywhere, would learn of his retreat to the peaceful countryside of the West Sussex Weald. The offer from an old army friend had been too good to pass up: help his ageing father to work the farm, in return for a small wage and a cottage to live in. The place needed repairs, but Revill would make a good fist of it. Since returning from the war in France in one piece, give or take a few scars, the former artillery captain was considered by many to be a lucky man.

'I know I must face him – Heneage,' he said at last. 'Though I did harbour hopes that, after my service in Normandy, he would leave me be.'

'You'll have to square it with Master Burwood,' Jenna said, turning to face him. 'There'll be the harvest to get in soon. He'll need every pair of hands he can get.'

Revill nodded. 'I'll pay for him to hire a man from the village, to take my place. I would never let Petrus down.'

'And I suppose I must turn milkmaid again, along with baking and brewing.'

He glanced at her, but saw no sign of resentment. Then, there seldom was with Jenna. It was well over a year since he had promised that he would never go to war again, and she knew him as a man of his word. But there was always the threat, the hold that the Vice-Chamberlain had over him: to call on him to undertake another mission, in which the soldier would likely have to turn spy again – a role he hated.

'I could take your embroideries with me to London,' he offered. 'To Stephens the haberdasher. You'll make a little money.'

She nodded. 'And doubtless you'll seek out Tom Bright, and get drunk.'

'Well, I might,' he answered. It was many months since he had seen his old gunnery corporal. 'Though I'm not even sure where he lives now.'

They were silent for a while. From the trees, rooks called as they settled to roost for the night. Finally she touched his arm, forcing him to turn.

'I'll wait until the end of September, Will. But no longer. We made vows, remember?'

'I'd hardly forget,' he said. 'But I can't be certain how long I'll be gone-'

'I know. But I won't spend another winter here - unless we're married.'

So, there it was: the matter that had lain unspoken between them for too long. There was nothing she wanted more than to be his wife, and he had sworn to it. But now... he met her eye, and saw a familiar look: one of determination, tinged with sadness.

'I'll see Petrus first thing tomorrow,' he said. 'I'll settle everything, then leave before mid-morning. Malachi needs the exercise – a fifty-mile ride will settle him.'

A RELUCTANT HERO

'I'll make up a pack,' was all Jenna said, before rising and going indoors.

Revill sat alone for a while, thinking over events. The Crown messenger had appeared the previous afternoon with a letter, ordering him to report to Heneage at Whitehall Palace within two days. There were no details, but there was a postscript suggesting that this would be the last mission Revill should undertake, after which the Vice-Chamberlain would consider his service completed. Even so, the summons filled Revill with foreboding. For some hours he had wrestled with the matter, thinking what excuses he might muster – but in the end, he knew it was to no avail.

For the spymaster still had a hold over him, on account of Revill's sister's conversion on marrying a Catholic. Now, a mere three years after the Armada, amid troubling rumours that Spain was already building up another fleet, even law-abiding Papists lived in fear of arrest. At times, he had wanted to curse the headstrong Katherine for her marriage – especially since she and her husband had lost the tenancy of their farm, and were facing poverty. Then he would recall her face, her dancing eyes, and his anger would melt away. He could do nothing but serve Heneage as ordered - no matter how many times he had cursed the smooth-voiced courtier to the very devil.

He emerged from his reverie to see that sun was almost gone. But as he rose, the notion struck him forcibly: this forthcoming mission, of which he knew nothing, might be the last straw as far as Jenna was concerned. She had always awaited his return: tended his wounds, fed him and bedded him, tolerated his ways. Now, if things went awry, he could even lose her - and no man, he thought, would blame her for it.

Let alone Revill himself.

***

Late the following afternoon, with red kites wheeling overhead, he walked his tired horse to the end of Long Southwark and paused at the Bridge gate, while the reek of London in high summer drifted across the Thames. Malachi scented it too, and tossed his head; they had both been away too long, in the sweet air of Sussex.

Now Revill berated himself: why had he come up through Southwark when he could have travelled via Richmond, or ridden to Lambeth and taken a boat?

'Old habits,' he muttered, leaning down to pat his old warhorse's neck. 'Let's forsake the stink of the city, shall we?' Upon which he turned Malachi about, retraced their steps and rode west, skirting noisy Bankside until he emerged on Lambeth Marsh. A short while later he had crossed the river by horse-ferry, dismounted and handed the reins to a boy before tramping through the King Street Gate into the rambling warren of Whitehall Palace. The interior was pleasantly cool after the warmth outside, yet he found a gloom settling upon him at the thought of facing Heneage again. He passed hurrying clerks, garishly-dressed courtiers and liveried guards, making his way to the room which he assumed was still occupied by the Vice-Chamberlain… only to receive a surprise.

'Sir Thomas has departed, along with most of the Privy Council,' a bad-tempered servant told him, as they stood in the passage. 'Surely you know The Queen has left on her Summer Progress?'

'As it happens, I didn't,' Revill said. 'I've been out of London for a while.'

'Her Majesty left Nonsuch Palace yesterday. She will stay first at Leatherhead, then move on to East Horsley, I believe. You might catch up with the Royal Party there.'

Revill eyed the man bleakly, not relishing another long ride out through Surrey. What was Heneage playing at, he wondered, ordering him to report here? Did he imagine that Revill troubled himself to keep abreast of Court matters? With a sigh, he glanced through the door of the empty chamber and was about to take his leave, when the clerk gave a start.

'One moment… what did you say your name was, again?'

Revill told him, whereupon the other put a hand to his forehead.

'Ah, yes… your pardon. I had forgotten. You'd best come with me – Captain Revill.'

With that the man led the way down the passage, rounding a corner and then another. Finally, on reaching a door, he knocked

A RELUCTANT HERO

and entered. Words were exchanged which Revill failed to hear, before the door was thrown wide and he was ushered in.

Across the surprisingly large room, beside a table untidy with scrolls and papers, propped up on cushions sat a small, hunched man in a black gown, with sharp eyes that met Revill's immediately. Though by the look of him he was under thirty years, he had the world-weary air of a much older person. Silently he waved the clerk away, waited for the door to close, then beckoned his visitor forward. Revill knew there was something familiar about the man, though he struggled to place him until he spoke.

'I am Sir Robert Cecil. You'll know who my father is.'

Of course... at once, he knew. Seated before him was the son of the Queen's celebrated First Secretary and longest-serving courtier, Lord Burghley, who was now past his seventieth year and said to be growing infirm. Revill had heard mention of the bookish son, reputed to be one of the finest minds in England - and who, he now recalled, had been taking on some of his father's duties. He approached, and made his bow.

'You came to see Sir Thomas Heneage,' Cecil said. 'You may attend me instead.'

Revill raised his brows and waited. The waiting went on until, growing uncomfortable, he was about to ask why he was here when the courtier pulled a paper out from under several others, scanned it briefly, then looked up.

'You have been warmly recommended to me,' he said, in a dry tone. 'Indeed, from what I've heard, your exploits would make a fine play for the theatres. Loyal, courageous and resourceful, carrying out the most dangerous of tasks...' Again, those piercing eyes bored into Revill's. 'Which makes me enquire, just what is it that makes you so devoted to the Vice-Chamberlain, that you indulge his every whim?'

Stuck for an answer, Revill found himself frowning. He was still searching for words when Cecil threw the paper down - and for the first time, allowed himself a faint smile.

'After all,' he went on, 'to my mind, Sir Thomas is not the sort of man who inspires unstinting loyalty, let alone devotion... would you concur in that?'

Revill cleared his throat. 'You put me at a disadvantage, sir,' he replied. 'And I fail to see why my opinions of the Vice-Chamberlain would interest you... no matter what they be.'

'Well, let's say that they are of interest,' Cecil said sharply. 'You may speak freely – you have my word upon it.'

For a moment, he suspected a trap of some sort. His mind whirling, he thought briefly of his dealings with the ruthless spymaster over the past two years – ever since the day he had walked, soaking wet, from the Artillery Ground to stand before Heneage's fire in his steaming clothes, to find himself blackmailed into carrying out his first, wretched mission for the man. It had been but the start of his unwilling service for the Vice-Chamberlain, who used him as an instrument... but now? He drew breath, and gave a nod.

'Very well, Sir Robert. Since you press me, I would rejoice wholeheartedly to be told I need never set eyes upon that man, ever again. And in truth, the only news I would desire to have of him thereafter would be word of his death.'

But when Cecil merely eyed him, his unease rose anew. At the back of his mind was the notion familiar to any old soldier: that he was in some sort of trouble, and had spoken rashly.

'You said I might speak freely,' he added.

'I did.' For a moment Cecil paused, as if thinking hard, then:

'Before I tell you what I want you to do for me, I would first hear your tale. For I see you're under Heneage's yoke, for some reason. In short, I do not believe you're a man who willingly undertakes the kind of missions my fellow Privy Councillor requires. As for wishing him gone from your life – that may not be so difficult to achieve. Does the thought cheer you?'

'By the Chri- I mean, it does,' Revill returned, almost blurting the words out. And though still uneasy, he felt a stirring of hope. In his mind's eye he saw Jenna, and imagined the joy it would bring them both, were he to be free...

'Then tell me, but make it brief,' Sir Robert Cecil said, growing brisk on a sudden. 'For I've other matters to attend to, before I join the Queen on her progress.'

And so Revill nodded, took a breath, and began.

A RELUCTANT HERO

In fact, it took him less time than he expected. He spoke of being called to Heneage's house in Seething Lane in the October of 1589, and given no choice but to embark on a mission to assassinate the eccentric country knight, Sir Abel Stanbury. The reasons for the assassination were murky, and would turn out to even murkier, but since he had been spared having to carry out the grisly deed, he chose not to dwell on the matter. Instead, he told of the reason he was forced to work for Heneage, on account of his young sister down in Devon who had married a Catholic and converted to Popery, and hence-'

'Ah, now I understand!'

Abruptly, Cecil cut him short. 'I knew there was something,' he went on. 'You were a reluctant assassin… and I gather from the report, that you were a reluctant traitor in France last year, posing as an emissary from the Catholic League.'

He paused, levelling a gaze at Revill that suggested – what? Approval, or even admiration? It struck him as unlikely. Finally he decided it was mere satisfaction, that his presence before this clever young courtier had not turned out to be a waste of his time – which would soon prove to be close to the truth.

'Well now, I will lay it forth,' Cecil said. 'I gather that Sir Thomas informed you this would be the last time he would call upon you to act… and yet, I suspect that knowing him as you do, you refused to believe it. Do I hit the mark?'

Revill managed a nod, and to his surprise, felt a smile coming on. From being highly suspicious of this man, he now found himself beginning to like him.

'So, we may proceed.' Suddenly, Cecil shifted in his chair and winced. It struck Revill that he was in some pain… the slight twist in his spine, perhaps? But his gaze remained steady, as the man delivered words that wiped away his smile in an instant.

'Serve me this one time, Revill, and you may forget about your obligation to your supposed spymaster,' he said flatly. 'Or did you think that, following Walsingham's death last year, Heneage now held all the cards?'

Revill met his gaze… and now, he was piecing things together. Like others, he had indeed believed that after Sir Francis

Walsingham had died in the April of 1590, intelligence matters had fallen to the Vice-Chamberlain. Lord Burghley was old, and becoming less nimble in regards to matters of state... but if his son was taking on some of the work, was he now the spymaster? After all, he had been knighted and, as he had revealed, been made a member of the Privy Council - most rare in one so young. Impressed, Revill spoke up.

'I did, sir. I heard rumours of a secret book that held Walsingham's details of all his intelligencers, with codes and ciphers, which I assumed had passed to Heneage – or indeed, to your father. But since that time-'

'I hold that book now,' Cecil broke in, without expression. 'And I intend to order matters somewhat differently to how they were ordered in the past. Though not quite yet...'

He looked aside briefly, before appearing to come to a decision. 'Well, enough of that. This is what I will charge you with, Revill: to join the train that follows the Queen on her Summer Progress. She means to pass through Surrey, and likely through part of Sussex, before arriving in Hampshire. She will visit Chichester and Portsmouth, and other places as the fancy takes her. As matters stand, she intends to be back by September... though by then, your task will likely be over.'

In silence, Revill could only stare at him.

'Come now,' his new spymaster said, raising an eyebrow. 'Surely you expected worse? I'm not asking you to kill anyone, or even to put your life in danger. It's a matter of quiet surveillance, and identifying a murderer before he can strike. You follow?'

'Strike - at whom?' Revill enquired.

'The Queen, of course,' came Cecil's reply. 'Who did you think?' Whereupon, seeing Revill dumbstruck, he let out a sigh.

'I will explain anon,' he continued. 'Doubtless you're thinking that Her Majesty is well-guarded, surrounded by courtiers and admirers, and welcomed by adoring crowds wherever she goes – all of which, of course, is true. But you'll also know the risks she runs, every time she ventures into the countryside. I've no need to remind you of the countless plots that have been laid against her, have I?'

A RELUCTANT HERO

'You have not, Sir Robert,' Revill answered, finding his voice. 'And yet, I'm uncertain-'

'Don't be,' the other broke in. 'Just be aware that, at this time, you are as trusted as any man I can think of to carry out the task I lay upon you. Moreover, you're unknown to those who surround the Queen, and able to mix with people of all classes.' He paused. 'Except that you won't – mix, that is. You will be part of a small party of men who have their own motives for being part of the retinue... and even there, you will find yourself set apart. Does the notion trouble you?'

'I suppose not,' Revill managed; the import of the matter was only now sinking in. Was he truly being asked to protect the Queen from an attempt on her life? But then, Cecil had spoken of the assignment being over by September, which would suit him well – and if this was to be his last such mission...

'In truth, I'm honoured, sir,' he added, keeping a level tone. 'I will do whatever I can.'

'I know you will,' Cecil replied. 'Had I thought otherwise, you would not be here.'

'Am I to go under a false name, as I did in Paris?' Revill asked then, as questions flew up. 'And a false profession, as I did the year before?'

'You may use whatever name you like,' came the swift reply. 'As for the profession...' the spymaster shrugged. 'That too, I'll leave to you. But make no mistake, Revill - whatever guise you assume, you will find you are an outsider.'

An outsider... Revill mulled over the word, and awaited his instructions.

TWO

He did not leave for Surrey that day; evening was already drawing in, and both he and Malachi needed rest before setting out in the morning. And after he had delivered Jenna's embroideries to the haberdasher there was only one place to go, as he had known all along: the home of Tom Bright. As for their getting pleasantly drunk, as he had promised his old corporal last year when they stood on a windy quayside in Dover: in view of what lay ahead, that would have to wait for another time. Yet despite the task that had been laid upon him - which he had tried to dismiss for the present - his spirits rose at the prospect of their meeting. Hence it was a disappointment, on reaching Bright's old lodgings in Dowgate, to find that he was not there.

'You mean, he's out?' He asked of the stout woman who stood in the doorway, looking him over unsmilingly. 'Which tavern does he frequent these days?'

'I mean he's quit his lodgings,' the woman said. 'And good riddance. I'll never let room to an old soldier again... he had no respect for my house, nor for anyone in it.'

Revill held his tongue. He was tired, and had no desire to embark on a defence of his old comrade - the most loyal man he knew - with his sour ex-landlady. He was turning away, resigned to finding an inn, when she stayed him.

'His old room is still free, though,' she said. 'If you were wanting a bed, as I think you are.' And when Revill raised his eyebrows, she added: 'There's rumours of plague, though I haven't heard of anyone catching it. No-one's sought lodging here for a while.'

'Very well,' he answered, since this would save some effort. 'But I'll only stay a night.'

The woman nodded and stood back to admit him. As he stepped into the passage, he asked her how long Tom Bright had been gone.

A RELUCTANT HERO

'More than a week, as I recall. Left in a hurry, too… but at least he settled his rent.'

'So he would,' Revill said, somewhat tartly. 'He's a good man.'

He followed his tight-lipped hostess up a narrow stair to a bare room at the rear of the house. Having handed her a coin, he waited to be left alone - but no sooner had she departed than he made a discovery.

The bed, he guessed - an ancient, rope-strung device with a torn and faded coverlet - had been untouched since Tom Bright had vacated it. But on glancing at the cover, he was surprised to see a tiny square of paper pinned to a corner. It would have been easy to miss it, or even to ignore it - which was likely Tom's intention, he realised. Four words had been scrawled on it which would mean nothing to another occupant of the room, but meant everything to Revill.

For Fiery Moll's Captain.

He stared at the words. *Fiery Moll* was the nickname of one of the two cannons Revill's gun crew had hauled across Northern France the previous year, before they took the Castle of Falaise – and which, under his command, they had later fired at the Battle of Ivry while serving in the French King's army. So - Tom Bright had guessed Revill would come looking for him sooner or later, as he had promised to do. More, he had counted on Revill wanting to see his old room to satisfy himself he was gone, or perhaps to look for clues as to his whereabouts. Standing beside the bed, Revill found a smile coming on as he thought of his wiry little corporal… and realised too, how much he had missed him.

'Well then, you clever old bastard,' he murmured to himself as he unpinned the scrap of paper. 'Let's hear what you had to say to me, before you took off.'

But on unfolding the missive, his smile faded as he read Bright's clumsily-formed words, with their somewhat erratic spelling.

I hope you finde this, Captain, else I've laboured for nort. Old foes caught up with me, so I hadd to take flyte. Catch me in Portsmouth if you want. I will seek shippe there, Deptford not safe. In trooth, England is not safe for me now. Your frend till deth, T B.

With the paper in hand Revill sank down on the bed, gazing at the initials.

***

After a meagre and hasty breakfast, he left Bright's old lodging-house at first light and was glad to put London behind him. With Malachi making good pace, he left the south gate of the Bridge and was soon passing through Newington on the road to Streatham, the Surrey hills rising to his left. With the familiar gait of the horse beneath him, he settled into the ride and at last allowed himself to think.

He thought first of his old corporal, and the troubling fact that Tom had felt obliged to make a retreat… but to Portsmouth? Tom was a Londoner, who would always look to the Thames as a potential route out of England. But then, if he believed it wasn't safe… it sobered Revill to think that one of the bravest men he knew might be in fear of his life. Then, with a frown, he recalled Sir Robert Cecil's words, when he had spoken of the Queen's Summer Progress as far as Hampshire, visiting Portsmouth among other places. It was possible, given what he now knew, that Revill might find himself there eventually.

It seemed a striking coincidence… or then again, perhaps it was merely the good fortune of the man his gun-crew had once dubbed Lucky Will Revill. Setting the matter aside, he turned his thoughts to the mission: the daunting task Cecil had laid upon him.

It was still a shock to think on it. It seemed there was a man, a peer of the realm no less, who had been kept under surveillance for the past three years – ever since the time of the Armada. A Catholic, though one of those who swore obeisance to the Crown, paid his recusancy fees and had never shown any sign of disloyalty, this man was following Queen Elizabeth on her Progress, as did so many nobles. Like the others he travelled with his own servants, and attended the Queen almost daily - which troubled Cecil a good deal.

This summer, it appeared, Elizabeth intended to visit a number of great houses held by Catholics, eager to demonstrate their loyalty to her. The shrewd old Queen, soon to turn fifty-eight years of age, wished to show not only that she had no fear of Papists in

A RELUCTANT HERO

her own country, but of the Spanish themselves, across the sea in the Low Countries where war still raged. Moreover, everyone knew that the lavish hospitality which was certain to be offered by such wealthy Catholics as Sir Anthony Browne, the master of Cowdray in Sussex, would save her considerable expense. When all was said and done, the parsimonious Elizabeth was a woman who delighted to be entertained and pampered. Thus far, all was as normal - apart from the presence of the man Revill was ordered to accompany throughout the Progress.

His name was Lord Ballater. Ennobled more than thirty years before, in the last days of Queen Mary, he was an old school Roman Catholic attended by Catholic servants. And, he was suspected of desiring a victory for the King of Spain. Worst of all, Cecil believed that Ballater would, at a moment of his choosing, contrive an attempt upon the life of the Queen.

'His train,' Cecil had said grimly, when Revill stood before him the previous afternoon. 'You'll need to watch every one of them like a hawk. I'm certain one is a varlet who's been brought in by Ballater to do the deed, before making his escape. Upon which, of course, His Lordship will appear as horrified as everyone else, and swear to hunt the man down. You must discover him before he can act.' Whereupon, when Revill showed consternation at the gravity of the task, he had added: 'You will not be entirely alone. I have people already in attendance, though you will not know them.'

His words were still running through Revill's head when he reached Cheam, and realised he was more than half way to Leatherhead.

***

By the time he reached the old town, around mid-day, as expected the great cavalcade that made up the Queen's Progress had already moved on: hundreds of people, along with their horses and dogs. Leatherhead was still buzzing with talk of the spectacle: the lords, knights, gentlemen and ladies in their fine clothes, the teeming servants, the two hundred ox-drawn carts carrying everything from jewellery to chamber-pots. They had filled the town as well as the homes of the local landowners, and spread far beyond it in tents and bivouacs. Byres had been emptied of cattle, barns emptied of hay, the stocks of bakers, butchers and fruiterers exhausted. People had stood all day to catch sight of Her Majesty, riding as was her custom instead of sitting in a coach. Skirting the top of the North Downs, her party had now rolled on to East Horsley where she was to be the guest of a wealthy gentleman, Thomas Cornwallis. Sir William Moore would be her host after that, at Losely near Guildford. The harbingers had long since gone ahead, to ensure that all was ready.

But Revill, following Cecil's instruction, would avoid all these places. His orders were to go to Farnham Castle and await the plodding Progress, which barely managed ten miles a day. When it arrived, he would present himself to Lord Ballater and show the letter of introduction Cecil had provided: to whit, to take this trusted ex-soldier into his service, on his personal recommendation.

As for Revill's profession, all he had to offer His Lordship were his fighting skills. After some swift consideration, Cecil had added a postscript to his letter to suggest that the former captain of artillery, who had done good service in France, would make an ideal bodyguard. Why Ballater might need the services of such a man, he left to his imagination. There was always danger in these troubled times – as there were hotheads eager to prove themselves before their Queen, by picking a fight with a known Papist.

So, to his discomfort, Revill was expected to guard Lord Ballater while identifying a potential assassin among his servants. Now, having considered the mission from all sides, he was tempted to curse himself for agreeing to undertake it.

Then once again, what choice had he?

***

At Leatherhead he rested only briefly, watering Malachi before riding on. It was twenty miles further west to Farnham, and he wanted to arrive before evening. In choosing his route, he was obliged to veer far to the south of the Royal Progress, by-passing it via Clandon and the hills of Blackheath before reaching Guildford. Once he had arrived, well ahead of the Queen's train, he would be able to relax and take a meal at an inn. Farnham would be crowded with people anticipating Elizabeth's arrival, among them petitioners hoping to catch her eye – for wherever Elizabeth went, with her went the seat of law and of government. The Privy Council would continue to conduct business throughout the Progress, Sir Robert Cecil among them. Though in that respect, Revill's orders were clear: he was to stay away from his new spymaster, who would ignore him.

The knowledge that Sir Thomas Heneage was also part of the travelling Council, however, made him uneasy: should he avoid his old spymaster too? Either way, he intended to do so.

Some hours later, sweaty and saddle-sore, he reached Farnham as the sun was beginning to sink, and drew Malachi to a halt before a horse-trough. The little town on the river Wey seemed tranquil enough, almost drowsy in the early evening. But on his way here he had passed travellers heading in this direction, people who knew what was about to descend upon the place. He glanced around, his eyes soon drawn to the castle, the country seat of the Bishop of Winchester which loured over the village: a great stone bulk, centuries old and still surrounded by its bailey wall. The Queen would take up residence there for a while, Cecil had told him, before crossing the nearby border into Hampshire.

Revill turned away, and set himself to seek more humble accommodation. He soon found himself at The Swan in West Street, where things started to become irksome. To begin with, he was told, he would have to share a chamber. All the inns were filling up, the landlord said, on account of the Queen's imminent arrival. Did the gentleman not know of it?

'I did,' Revill answered, eying a ruddy-faced, cheerful man who was clearly savouring the prospect of an increase in business. 'So, how many must I share with?'

'Only one, sir - thus far, that is,' came the reply. 'Yet it could become two, or even three… there's no room for more. Unless, that is…' He grinned. 'Unless your worship cares to bespeak the whole chamber for yourself? I would have to charge for four, but you look like a man of means – what say you?'

'I'll share with one other,' Revill told him, not relishing the stink of three other bodies in a cramped space: the Swan was not a large inn. Cecil had provided him with a heavy enough purse, but he had no wish to deplete it so soon. He had a suspicion that the price for his bed and board, as well as Malachi's stabling, was already inflated on account of the approaching Progress.

'As you wish,' the landlord beamed. 'The other gentleman is abroad just now, but will no doubt return for supper. Will you dine, too?'

'I will,' Revill replied. 'What's the name of my chamber-fellow?'

'Nicholas Godwin, sir. He's a Crown Purveyor – an important man just now, of course. I'm sure you'll get along. And my name is Hickes – whatever you need, I pray you, ask me or my wife and it shall be yours.'

'For now, shall we say a bowl of warm water and a ball of soap?' Revill said. Upon which, as Master Hickes hurried off to comply, he made his way to the stairs. But as he climbed, a frown creased his brow. So, this man Godwin was a Crown Purveyor: one of those unpopular officials charged with buying up supplies for the Queen and her followers - often at dismally low prices. And, the landlord was sure he and Revill would *get along*?

He had doubts about that – and when supper-time arrived, and he and his new chamber-fellow sat down to eat in the Swan's crowded parlour, he was soon proved right.

***

Godwin was a rogue, and a sly one at that: Revill knew it within minutes of meeting him. The man's opening words were: 'I got to the room first, my friend, so I've taken the bed by the window. You'll do well enough on the truckle, yes? I don't snore - or so I'm told. Then, you can't believe everything whores tell you. Speaking of which, do you mind if I bring one up to the chamber, now and then? Not a Puritan, are you?'

'I'm not,' Revill answered. 'But I do like to get a night's sleep.'

For reply, the other put on a bland look. After their brief exchange, the two of them had descended the stairs and found a table, surrounded by talkative countrymen quenching their thirst after a day's work. August was drawing on, and the harvest had already begun here. Revill was at ease among such folk – but Godwin, it seemed, was not.

A RELUCTANT HERO

'By the Christ,' he muttered, glancing about. 'What a parcel of oafs. All of a sudden, I find myself glad of your company, sir. Your name, again?'

'Thomas Perrot,' Revill replied, having decided to use the cover name he had been given the year before, on the secret mission to Paris.

'And what's your business, Perrot?

'Does it matter?' Revill returned.

'Well, not much. But since you're a stranger here like me, I expect your presence is on account of the Queen's coming. Petition, is it? You don't look like a mere gawper.'

'I'm hired to attend someone,' Revill told him, not wishing to say more. Fortunately, a slim, fair-faced woman in an apron appeared just then with their supper. As she set down the platters, Godwin looked up with a broad grin.

'Mistress Hickes! How pleasant to see you this evening. Are you well?'

The hostess, somewhat flustered, forced a smile. 'I am, Master Godwin. Is there anything more you require – or you, sir? Master Perrot, is it not?'

She turned deliberately to Revill, who understood why. She needed a diversion from the attentions of Godwin – as predatory a man as he had seen in a long while.

'It is, and all is well,' he replied. 'We won't detain you… a busy time, no?'

'That it is, sir, and soon to get busier.' Mistress Hickes threw a sidelong glance at his chamber-fellow. 'I'll have time for naught but work and sleep – as will my husband.'

'Such a pity,' Godwin said, maintaining his grin. 'I had a mind to invite you-'

'Shall we eat?' Revill broke in. 'I'm famished - and our hostess has others to attend to.' Favouring her with a kindly look, he added: 'Perhaps you'll take my mug and refill it?'

He held out his tankard, which Mistress Hickes saw was still half-full. But she took it without a word, nodded and moved away.

'Well now, I see you spoke truly when you said you were no Puritan,' Godwin said, with what could only be described as a leer.

'Set your sights on her too, have you? So, what say you to a wager, as to which of us beds her first?'

Revill gave a sigh, and merely shook his head.

***

The next morning, he awoke on the narrow truckle-bed with sunlight flooding the chamber. Across the room Godwin snored, as he done for much of the night despite his claims to the contrary. Getting to his feet, Revill looked about for the chamber-pot. Then he heard noises through the open window: it sounded like a disturbance. He stepped across the room in his hose, leaned across the slumbering form of his fellow and peered out. They were at the front of the inn, overlooking the street, but all looked peaceful enough as far as Revill could see.

He was turning aside - when there came a cry from only inches away, and in an instant Godwin had jerked awake, seized his wrist and clenched it in a fierce grip. At the same time, he thrust a hand under his pillow and produced a poniard, fumbling it by the hilt.

'For pity's sake!' Grabbing the other's forearm, Revill shook him harshly. 'You're dreaming – wake yourself!'

With a gasp Godwin opened his eyes wide, then fell back. His face was haggard, with none of the brazen confidence he had shown the previous evening. Letting go of Revill's wrist, he let out a breath.

'Your pardon… I forgot myself…'

'So I observe,' Revill said, releasing him in turn. 'Expecting trouble, were you?' He nodded towards the poniard, which Godwin quickly lowered.

'A man in my position must take precautions,' he said, after a moment. 'I, er-'

'Make enemies?' Revill broke in, stepping away from the bed. 'Well, that doesn't surprise me much, given what you do.'

'How do you know what I do?' The other demanded, sitting up. 'I never vouchsafed it.'

'Hickes told me. He considers you an important man, I understand.'

'Unlike you,' came the retort. But when Revill frowned, he added: 'I mean, you don't consider me important - is it not so?'

A RELUCTANT HERO

'I'll reserve judgement,' Revill said.

'What in God's name were you doing, standing over me?' Godwin asked then. But when Revill merely nodded towards the window, from where noise persisted, he turned to listen.

'It's only the market,' he muttered. 'Market day in Farnham... perhaps I'll take a sojourn about the place later. Would you care to accompany me?'

'I think not,' Revill said, turning away to resume his hunt for the chamber-pot. 'I prefer the company of my horse.'

And a short time later, having breakfasted alone, he was walking out into the sunlight. Soon he had greeted Malachi in the Swan's stables, finding him well-fed and content, and was preparing to ride forth to make a sojourn of his own.

He had to pass the time somehow. It would be several more days before the Queen's train reached Farnham. Just now, however, he had an urge to disobey Cecil's instruction and ride eastward to meet it, perhaps at Losely. The thought of having to put up with Godwin for much longer irked him considerably.

But in the end, he rejected the notion. On a sudden, he realised he was in no hurry to present himself to Lord Ballater, and commence what could be the most difficult mission he had ever undertaken... even, perhaps, the most dangerous.

As he led Malachi out of the stable, he thought of Jenna at work on the farm, and envied her.

THREE

Three days passed, by which time Farnham's population had grown considerably. Like every other inn the Swan was now bursting at the seams, and Revill was glad he and Godwin had a room to themselves. His chamber-fellow, seemingly not short of money, had even agreed to split the cost equally, which went some way towards Revill tolerating his presence along with his tiresome behaviour. But as they shared breakfast on a cloudy morning, which held the threat of a summer shower, Godwin surprised him by making a proposition.

'As a rule, I have a servant to assist me,' he said, through a mouthful of porridge. 'But I had to dismiss the fellow some time ago… a matter of insolence. Yet my work is taxing, and I would value your help. I can pay a shilling a day – so, what say you?'

'I say no,' Revill replied, after a short pause. 'I told you, I'm to attend a nobleman who will arrive with the Queen.'

'There are other benefits, beside the fee,' Godwin said, putting on one of his sly looks. 'Some people – poor farmers, for example - can't bear to part with their animals, or their fodder, let alone their food stocks. Yet since they have little choice in the matter, they'll do almost anything to… to come to other terms, shall I say?' And when Revill frowned, he added: 'I speak of even offering the services of their wives or daughters - do you see?'

'I do,' Revill replied. 'I also see why men like you are despised, the length and breadth of England. I wonder if the Queen truly knows what her Purveyors get up to.'

'I doubt if she'd care, whether she knew or not,' Godwin retorted, waving his spoon in the air. 'By the Christ, Perrot, you can be a sanctimonious cove at times.'

'I can be a bad-tempered cove, too,' Revill told him. 'Soldiering does that to a man, didn't you know?'

'So, you were a soldier,' came the sharp reply. 'Not quite a true gentleman, eh?'

A RELUCTANT HERO

'Not quite,' Revill returned. 'And I'd advise you not to press me too far, and find out.'

'What, is that a threat?' Godwin snapped. 'Have a care, my friend. Very soon now we will be on the Verge – within seven miles of the Queen's presence, in case I need remind you. An assault, or even a threat, against a Crown servant would be deemed an attack on Her Majesty herself – and punishable by death. You'd do well to remember that, when you...'

But he trailed off as, with an air of disregard, Revill dabbed his mouth with a napkin, threw it down and stood up abruptly.

'Have a pleasant day foraging, or whatever else you mean to do,' he said. Whereupon, allowing his hand to fall briefly to his sword-hilt, he turned and made his way through the crowded parlour. The place resembled an obstacle course nowadays, due to the extra tables Hickes had squeezed in. It was abuzz with voices, but Revill paid them no mind. He was about to go outside when Mistress Hickes appeared at his elbow.

'By heaven, Master Perrott,' she breathed, looking flustered. 'It's almost upon us – have you heard?'

With a shake of his head, Revill asked what it was he hadn't heard.

'The Queen, sir. The word is, her train will pass through Seale before mid-day. That's less than three miles off – she'll be here this afternoon! What joy, eh?'

'Why, yes.' Revill smiled. 'A joyous day indeed.'

'Some folk have gone forth already, to line the road,' Mistress Hickes added. 'Not for years has Farnham seen such a sight - will you ride out yourself?'

'Well, I believe I will,' Revill said. 'Let's hope the rain holds off, shall we?'

But his hostess was already moving away. And such was the excitement he sensed as he stepped outside into the street, he doubted if even a heavy shower could dampen the spirits of Farnham's residents.

The Royal Progress was approaching... and Revill, to his growing unease, was about to become a part of it. Drawing a breath, he headed off to the stables to saddle Malachi.

JOHN PILKINGTON

***

So at last, the great host arrived, somewhat later in the afternoon than expected. There had indeed been a shower of rain, which had mudded the roads and slowed the cavalcade down. But by the time the first riders appeared at the edge of the town, the sun was out again. And finally, to a chorus of shouting and cheering, Queen Elizabeth herself arrived amid a host of courtiers and attendants, resplendent in their finery.

Near the castle entrance, Revill stood beside his horse and watched. He saw the advance guards ride by, well-armed and alert. Officials in their gowns followed, sweating in the heat, before the Queen herself arrived, riding a white mare. At that moment, with perfect timing, a welcoming party appeared from the castle, led by the Bishop of Winchester himself. Florid speeches followed, until some of the courtiers, eager to get unhorsed and indoors, began to show impatience. But Elizabeth herself, in a finely-embroidered riding cloak, was the picture of serenity as she sat her horse and acknowledged the tributes.

Revill had seen her before, in London, from a distance. But it struck him now, as he recalled Sir Robert Cecil's words of a few days before, how exposed the Queen was on such occasions as this. A man could dart from the crowd and assail her before the guards could stay him... but here in Farnham, there was only adulation. Townspeople, crowding about on all sides, doffed hats and listened eagerly to the fine words, though precious few would understand the Latin. *Gawpers*, Godwin had dubbed them... and just now, Revill realised, he was one of them.

Whereupon he caught sight of a familiar figure among the assembled noblemen, and turned quickly aside. Sir Thomas Heneage, still cloaked from the rain, sat on a fine chestnut horse, observing the proceedings with what looked to Revill like indifference bordering on irritation.

And now he saw Sir Robert Cecil - moreover, he realised, the man had seen him. Sitting close to the Queen with other members of her Council, the little hunchback threw a sharp glance in Revill's direction before looking away. But it was enough: Cecil knew that his man was here, and ready to carry out his mission.

A RELUCTANT HERO

Feeling restless, Revill waited until the speeches were done and the party had begun to enter the Castle. There were cheers, waving of hats and cries of 'God save your Majesty!' from the crowd. Following that, it was some time before the rear guard, along with a few covered carts, had clattered past, leaving others outside to find their own accommodation. But already he had guessed that Lord Ballater's party was not among the stragglers. Perhaps the man preferred to keep apart... turning away, he eased Malachi through the throng, which showed no sign of dispersing. Finally he was able to get clear, whereupon he mounted and urged the horse to a trot, heading eastwards until he was almost out of Farnham. And still the train of heavy baggage carts rolled in, drawn by plodding oxen, as far ahead as he could see. Beside them trudged the humbler servants who would soon be putting up tents, unhitching beasts and unloading wagons in the heat.

Finally, seeing a guard in livery, Revill reined in and hailed the man, asking if he knew the whereabouts of Lord Ballater's train. Fortunately, an answer came readily enough.

'Old Ballater?' The soldier squinted up at him. 'He's lodging at a house a mile back, on the road to Seale. But as for his train...' He gave a shrug. 'There's but three men with him, and one half-blind at that. The man's too tight-fisted to hire more, from what I've heard.'

He moved on, leaving Revill to mull over what he had said. Three men? It seemed a very small party for a peer of the realm to bring along; then again, if one of them was a hired assassin, as Cecil feared, it might make Revill's task somewhat easier...

He shook the rein and urged Malachi forward, his mind busy with the task ahead. At least, he told himself, he should be able to move out of the Swan and quit Godwin's company.

***

The dwelling turned out to be an old farmhouse, somewhat rundown but spacious enough. The farm was gone, the land sold save for a stable and a chicken-house. But the farmer's widow had stayed, taking in guests when occasion served. Just now she seemed more than willing to accommodate Lord Ballater and his followers, and Revill soon realised why: the woman was a

Catholic, white-haired and black-clad, of the same generation as His Lordship. There was even a large crucifix on the wall, in plain view. Revill ignored it when he entered the house, greeting her politely. He was in a wide, low-beamed room, with doors leading off.

'His Lordship occupies the best chamber, sir, upstairs,' she said in answer to his question. 'But he's resting after his ride... might I ask what business you have with him?'

She looked wary, which was unsurprising. Keen to put her at ease, Revill explained that he was ordered to guard Lord Ballater. And might he know whom he was addressing?

'I'm Rebecca Bradby,' the widow told him. 'Do you mean you'll want to stay here, along with the other men?'

'If I may, Mistress,' Revill answered. 'I'm none too fussy where I bed down...'

He stopped at the sound of footsteps, coming from the rear of the house. Looking past Rebecca Bradby he saw a heavy-set man in good clothes, blocking the doorway. Hatless and sunburnt, he eyed Revill stonily.

'Who are you?' He demanded.

'My name's Perrot,' Revill said. 'I'm to serve your master – that is, assuming you're one of Lord Ballater's men? I have a warrant.' He took it from his doublet and held it up.

'Serve him?' The man took a step forward. 'In what fashion?'

'That's something I'll discuss with His Lordship, if it please you,' Revill told him. But when the other frowned, he thought it wise to assert himself from the outset. 'Or, even if it doesn't please you,' he added. 'You'll soon learn why.'

'I will, will I?' The other retorted. 'So, why not tell me now? My master's at rest, and won't wish to be disturbed.'

But at that, Mistress Bradby intervened. With a frosty look, she turned and addressed the man in forthright terms, informing him that hers was a godly house, and she expected her guests to act in seemly fashion. Revill's opinion of her rose considerably.

'It's best that I attend His Lordship at once,' he said. 'My charge comes from the Privy Council... he will receive me, I'm sure.'

A RELUCTANT HERO

Turning to the hostess, he added: 'And I swear to act in seemly fashion while I am under your roof.'

'Well… as you wish, sir,' came the reply. 'Though I expect Master Harman will want to accompany you. He is-'

'I'm Lord Ballater's steward,' the man in question broke in. 'And I'd like to see that letter you carry before we go up… if it pleases you, that is,' he added with sarcasm.

Revill sighed, and gave a nod. And a few minutes later, the two of them were mounting the stairs and approaching a door at the end of the landing. Harman the steward tapped, waited for an answering voice, then entered. Without waiting for invitation Revill followed – to come to an abrupt halt.

Having had no description of this lord who was the subject of Sir Robert Cecil's suspicions, he was unsure what to expect, save that Ballater was widowed and elderly. But the man he saw sprawled by the window in a low chair, his enormous bulk further padded by an old-fashioned gown, took him by surprise. The florid face, framed by a snowy beard, turned at his approach, the heavy eyebrows lifting like a pair of white mice. Hands like shovels rested on his knees, rings so embedded in the fleshy fingers they could never be removed. Revill, letter in hand, kept silent while Master Harman bent low to his master and spoke a few words.

'By heaven… is it so?' His Lordship's gaze moved from his steward to Revill. 'Come hither, man, and let me see you!'

Revill came forward, made his bow and spoke briefly, presenting his credentials. Ballater, however, made no effort to take the letter, only frowned at what he clearly considered an intrusion. Glancing at his steward, he demanded to know if the unloading was finished. Harman spoke in the affirmative, adding that supper would soon be prepared. Would His Lordship have it sent up to his chamber, or…?

'I'll think on it,' came the reply. And when the man hesitated, Ballater waved him away.

Harman went out, throwing Revill a hard look as he passed. For his part, Revill kept his face free of expression and waited until he was gone. He had time to look round and observe the room, hung with old embroideries of biblical scenes. Beside the four-poster bed, chests waited to be unpacked. Turning to his new master, he realised he was still holding up the letter of recommendation.

'Well then, let me have it,' Ballater growled, stretching out his hand.

Revill watched him read it, slowly and laboriously. It struck him that the man's eyesight was poor, which reminded him of words spoken to him on the road, about one of his servants being half-blind... at which moment, Ballater lowered the paper and gave a snort.

'By the saints, Cecil urges me to take a bodyguard, does he?' He grunted. 'How considerate, this sudden concern for my well-being... while there was I, thinking that little imp would like nothing more than to see me dead! Me, and every other follower of the true religion which he despises. We're agents of Spain, are we not – vipers, every one of us!'

Standing in silence, Revill remained straight-faced.

'And what of you... Perrot?' His Lordship demanded, flourishing the letter. 'I read that you're highly regarded - a war-hero of some kind. Which prompts me to ask who you fought for... do you care to answer?'

'I fought for the Queen's army, my Lord,' Revill replied. 'And I slew Spaniards, if that's the way your mind moves. Thought I might add that it was nothing personal.'

Ballater regarded him for a moment. 'And your service to me - provided I take you into it, of course – would that not be personal?'

'I was ordered to guard you, sir, and will do so with my life,' Revill told him. 'You attend Her Majesty, and like the rest of her subjects you deserve nothing less.' He paused, then: 'However, in the matter of religion I have no opinion, nor is it my place to think on such. I'm a sword for hire... I merely hope that you'll not need me to draw it.'

Another moment passed, then: 'My steward thinks you may be a spy,' Ballater said quietly.

'Then he's mistaken, my Lord,' Revill answered, as levelly as he could.

'Yet it's in his nature to be suspicious,' the other went on, as if he hadn't heard. 'He is of my faith, as are the rest of my servants.

A RELUCTANT HERO

They would resent your presence, and treat you always as a stranger - even a heretic. You understand me, I think.'

'That's of no consequence, sir,' Revill answered, after a pause. 'My orders are to look to your safety. The Queen's Progress has many miles to travel, I understand, even as far as the South Coast. With our troops still engaged across the Channel in France, feelings run high in certain quarters... I think Your Lordship will take my meaning?'

'Of course I do, man – and your tone lacks respect,' came the reply. 'Do you assume that my own servants are incapable of defending me, should any threat arise? For Cecil appears to do so,' Ballater added. 'Which – as I've said already - makes me wonder.'

Following which exchange, they both fell silent.

'And still...' With a heavy sigh, His Lordship lowered his eyes. 'What choices does a pauper have,' he murmured, almost to himself. 'I don't trust you, but if you're as good as your word, mayhap I shouldn't need to. You'll look to yourself, I take it, and expect nothing from me?'

'Of course, my Lord,' Revill said.

'Then leave me, for now. And tell Harman I'll take supper here. Meanwhile, you'd best acquaint yourself with my other servants – Hawkins and Dickon, their names. Dickon's eyesight is very poor, as you'll discover.'

And with that, the meeting was done. Revill made his bow and went out, glancing back as he closed the door to see the ageing lord close his eyes and slump in his chair.

Somehow, he did not strike Revill as a potential regicide; rather a gone-to-seed nobleman from another age, with little apart from memories to sustain him - along with his faith.

***

That evening he sat down to supper in the farmhouse with Ballater's servants, and took pains to observe them. Harman he had already assessed as a blustering fellow, somewhat bullying but probably harmless, his devotion to his master beyond question. Hawkins turned out to be a leathery ex-soldier, one of the rank-and-file who, a year or so back, would have been under the command of an officer like Revill. He had the hunted look common enough to men of his stamp: glad enough to have employment, but trusting no-one. Yet, like Harman he seemed an unlikely threat... which left Dickon, the youngest. And in a very short time, Revill came to a conclusion that aroused his suspicion: namely, that the man was not nearly as poor-sighted as he pretended.

For Revill had seen blind men aplenty: in the aftermath of battles, in the army hospitals, in the streets of London and Paris - and to his mind, they generally fell into two camps. Either they made great show of their infirmity, begging for charity, or they took pains to do the opposite: strive to master it, to prove that they were as capable as the next man. Dickon, pale-complexioned and thin-bearded, did neither. Instead, he had the air of a serious young gentleman, perhaps a third or fourth son who had been prepared to take a lowlier station in life. His duties, it seemed, amounted to little more than fetching and carrying, attending Lord Ballater of an evening and being on hand as a body-servant. Having made his introductions and found all three men cool towards him, Revill made an effort to converse.

'I've no knowledge of how long we'll stay here,' Harman said, in answer to his question. 'Could be two days, or even a week. What's your interest?'

'Call it idle curiosity,' Revill answered. 'In truth, it makes no difference to me.'

A brief silence followed, which Dickon chose to fill.

'From Farnham, the Queen intends to move south to a place called Bramshott,' he said, with a vague glance in Revill's direction. His voice was soft, with no accent. 'Though she changes her mind sometimes... a sore trial to her Councillors. Fickleness, thy name is woman, eh?'

The others said nothing, but busied themselves with the supper Mistress Bradby had provided.

'I can't help but think this is a small train His Lordship travels with,' Revill said in a casual tone. 'Are there many more servants, back at his home?'

'Why do you ask that?' Hawkins demanded. They were the first words he has spoken since sitting down at table. 'More idle curiosity, is it?'

'If you like,' Revill said, meeting what he saw was a threatening look.

'That can get a man into trouble, where I come from,' the ex-soldier said. 'And before you ask where that is, I won't tell. More, I'd prefer it if you kept out of my way henceforth. Do that, and we'll get along well enough - you follow?'

'Well enough,' Revill said, after a pause. He shifted his gaze to Harman, who looked up from his platter. 'I'm not here to make friends,' he added, 'but to guard His Lordship - a precaution the Queen's Council deem necessary. That's not to cast doubt on any of you men, of course… but in these times, one can't be too careful, can one?'

Whereupon, in the cold silence that followed, he turned attention to his meal and did not look up again. And if he sensed the hostility of all his table companions, he gave no sign.

But as he ate, his mind was active. Three men… one of whom, if Sir Robert Cecil's fears had foundation, was here to make an attempt upon the Queen's life: was it truly possible? For on first impressions at least, none of them looked to him like a potential assassin.

But if one of them had stirred his suspicions, it was the mild-mannered Dickon. Those who strove to appear the last offensive, he had found, were often the ones to watch.

FOUR

The Queen remained at Farnham Castle for several days – and by the end of her stay, Revill had almost lost track of time. He knew it was almost mid-August, but his routine in Lord Ballater's service was so dull, his opportunities to engage with others so few, that one day at the farmhouse seemed very like another. Save, that was, for the Sabbath when it came, marking a change of behaviour on the part of His Lordship and his servants. So that, when he was asked to ride out and exercise the party's horses, he guessed why: they were holding a private service – and Revill, the only non-Catholic, was not wanted.

He should have expected it, he realised. There was a distance between him and the other men that was unbreachable - and as for Ballater himself, the man hardly ever addressed him. Most days the old lord rode into Farnham to make a show of attending the Queen which, Revill suspected, was nothing more than that: a show. As far as he knew there were no other Papist noblemen on the Progress, though some would play host to it later – particularly at the great house of Cowdray, fifteen miles to the south. If there was indeed danger to Elizabeth, Revill had a notion that it might well arise in the vicinity of that manor, a notorious meeting place for Catholics. Some even dubbed it 'Little Rome', and spoke of priests hidden within the house, hearing confessions and conducting secret masses.

Such thoughts were on his mind when he took the party's mounts from the stables, along with Malachi. As a rule the horses were looked after by Hawkins, helped sometimes by Dickon who, Revill had already decided, moved about with more alacrity than he would expect in one who was almost blind. One of his duties was to assist the other men in getting Lord Ballater mounted on his horse, closer in build to a carthorse than any other breed - no easy task, given His Lordship's weight. It took all three of them to accomplish it, which had caused Revill some private amusement the first time he witnessed it. Thereafter, his own place was to ride close behind his new master, who ignored him, and wait for him whenever he chose to pass the time of day with other dignitaries. But such times were few, and the man never dismounted until he had ridden back to the farmhouse.

Quite why he was on the Progress at all, in fact, had begun to prey on Revill's mind, for he appeared to take little pleasure in it; perhaps Cecil had reason to suspect his motives after all.

It was a sunny morning when he led the horses out into the road behind Malachi, strung in a line. Along with the sturdy Suffolk workhorse that drew the company's baggage-cart, Lord Ballater's heavy mount was the slowest, obliging him to keep a modest pace. Once out in open country he turned the animals loose, allowing them to frolic in the sunshine and graze for a while. Sitting in the shade of a tree while Malachi cropped grass nearby, his thoughts turned to Jenna... and thence to Cecil's promise, that this would be his last mission. Heneage, he refused to think on - even if the man were barely a mile away from where he sat. Hope, he knew, was what sustained him, and made him keep to his resolve. Somehow, he must discover whether one of Ballater's men truly posed a threat to the Queen's life; the consequences of failure were unthinkable.

The matter was still in his thoughts when he returned to Mistress Bradby's, and learned that preparations were in progress to move out - that very morning. It seemed The Queen had already bidden farewell to Farnham, and intended to reach Bramshott in a single day's travel.

'I'll need you to lend a hand with the loading, Perrot,' Harman said, in something of a sweat. 'This may seem like a holiday to you, but it isn't for the rest of us.'

Revill said nothing, but went indoors to help bring His Lordship's belongings out. For a while all was bustle, with some muttered curses at the hurried departure. Finally, when everything was stowed on the cart and covered, the carthorse in the traces and the party set to leave, Ballater himself came out of the house with Dickon and Mistress Bradby... whereupon something occurred that made Revill start. It was but a brief gesture, which might well have gone unnoticed by a less observant man than he, yet it was striking – indeed, a revelation.

What had passed between the rest of the company that morning, while he was away, he could only guess. And when the hostess bobbed low before Lord Ballater, he thought it merely a mark of respect... until he saw Dickon, standing beside his master, place a hand on the woman's head and murmur something inaudible. And at once Revill knew what it meant – as he knew what function the young man fulfilled in Ballater's train.

Dickon was a priest in disguise, who was giving the devout Mistress Bradby his blessing.

At once, he turned aside and busied himself with Malachi's trappings, adjusting the saddle-girth. Thoughts raced through his mind, but he kept his head bent low. Hawkins was clambering up on to the cart, taking the reins. But Harman was standing nearby... Revill risked a glance, before deciding that he had not seen him observe what had passed.

'Let's not delay any longer, you men!' His Lordship called out, with forced heartiness. 'The Queen is on the road already... will you get me horsed?'

With Hawkins manning the cart, Revill was obliged to assist as Ballater walked heavily to his mount and waited to be helped into the saddle. That done, the party at last set forth, hooves throwing up a dust as they moved out of the farmyard. Looking back, he saw Mistress Bradby watching them depart: an upright, black-clad figure. For a moment, he believed she was about to cross herself.

Thereafter, nobody spoke as the little cavalcade travelled through Farnham, to bring up the rear of Queen Elizabeth's Progress as it rolled due south, towards Bramshott.

***

The journey was hot, slow and tedious. Revill rode close behind His Lordship, with Harman leading the party and Dickon beside the cart, seemingly to keep pace. But his secret was out now, which put a new light on everything. A priest, in Ballater's train, under the eyes of almost everyone? The boldness of the man – let alone his courage – almost took Revill's breath away. Were he discovered, he would be in irons within minutes and destined for

A RELUCTANT HERO

a harsh questioning, before facing almost certain execution - while the consequences for His Lordship could barely be imagined

And yet, the discovery threw up more questions. The clandestine priests, the bane of fiercely Protestant Councillors like Cecil, carried out forbidden acts - yet they were men of peace, who did no violence to anyone. Already some of them had gone willingly to the gallows, praying and affirming their faith to their last breath - especially the Jesuits: few in number, but tireless in their fanatical mission to restore Catholicism to England. They employed disguise when travelling, of course, as did Dickon; now, there was no doubt in Revill's mind that the young man had held mass at the farmhouse while he had been absent.

One fact, however, rose clearly: Dickon, or whatever his true name was, may have been an impostor yet he was no assassin; such a deed would be anathema to him. Which of the others, then, should Revill suspect - the taciturn Hawkins, or the blustering Harman?

All day the matter preyed on his mind as they passed through green pasture, descending the gentle southern slopes of the North Downs. Sheep grazed the fields, countrymen paused on the road to watch the great procession pass. Occasionally a messenger rode by, and once a pair of guards in royal livery came up from the main body of the Progress, seemingly looking out for stragglers. Revill caught a look of displeasure on the face of one when he eyed Lord Ballater, but it was gone as both men acknowledged His Lordship respectfully enough. Thereafter they turned and rode back, prompting Harman to mutter under his breath.

'What's that, master steward?' Ballater enquired, turning laboriously in the saddle, his face flushed in the afternoon heat. Keeping one hand on the rein, with the other he drew a kerchief from his sleeve and mopped his forehead.

Harman eased his mount closer to His Lordship's. 'Those men came but to check on us, my Lord – no other reason,' he said. 'The closer we get to Cowdray, the more alert they become.'

'Well, what matter if they do?' His master replied. 'We keep apart, and give no cause to draw attention… is that not so, Perrot?'

Ballater had shifted his gaze to Revill who, surprised at being addressed at all, answered without thinking. 'Indeed, sir... you are a model of good behaviour,' he said. Whereupon, seeing the frosty look that appeared on the steward's face, he added: 'To put up with the dust of the baggage carts as you do back here, I mean. It shows a loyalty much to be admired.'

'Are you trying to be amusing, Perrot?' Harman demanded, looking sharply at him.

'Of course not,' Revill replied. 'Why would I?'

They exchanged looks briefly, but the moment passed. Puffing like a drayhorse, Lord Ballater was peering ahead into the haze, and gave a start.

'By the saints, they're stopping at last,' he breathed. 'Time for meat and drink - Hawkins! Halt the cart, and we'll take our ease... let's pray the ale's not too warm, eh?'

At which, with relief, the party moved off the road and slowed to a stop. The Queen, it appeared, had ordered a rest, and men and beasts alike were eager for sustenance. As he dismounted Revill glanced pointedly at Dickon, but the other gave no sign of noticing. Nor did he speak throughout their rest-time – to Revill, or to anyone else.

And a few hours later, as the afternoon waned, Her Majesty's Progress finally arrived at Bramshott Place, the seat of Elizabeth's next host Sir Edmund Mervyn. There would be speeches of welcome, and presentation of gifts, and warm words of thanks from the sovereign... but Lord Ballater's party saw none of it. Instead, given the shortage of accommodation, his servants were soon busy erecting tents for the duration, and foraging for supplies to provide supper. Mercifully, they learned that this was to be a stay of a single night, before the Queen's train crossed into West Sussex and reached the fabled Cowdray.

In fact, Revill realised, having travelled in a great arc since leaving London a week ago, he was back within a few miles of Burwood's farm - and of Jenna. Whereupon a scheme sprang to mind that he was unable to resist.

And that night, while Ballater's company slept soundly in their tents, he stole out of the temporary camp, led Malachi away and saddled him swiftly and silently. Within minutes he was mounted and riding by the light of a half-moon, to be with his betrothed.

It took him more than an hour to cover the distance in near-darkness, and on two occasions he believed he was lost. But at last he found himself on the road to the tiny village of Chiddingfold, and recognised the terrain. From there it was a short distance to Burwood's farm, where he dismounted before his cottage. A moment later he was inside, closing the door and calling out softly, to be greeted by a startled cry from above.

Then came hurried footsteps on the stair, and she was in his embrace.

***

In the hour before dawn, having slept like a corpse, he was woken by Jenna speaking his name. Blearily he peered about, then let out a groan.

'You should leave, before Lord Whatever-his-name-is finds you gone,' she murmured.

'I know…' Sitting up, he took her face in his hands and kissed her. 'I had to see you, and let you know where I'm bound for. Though I know not when the mission will be done.'

'I'll wait,' she said. 'But don't tell me not to fret, for I can do no other. It looks to me as if you've been sent into a firestorm, with not even a cup of water to staunch the flames.'

He had no reply to that; having sat up half the night before going to bed, he had told her everything. Given their last conversation before he had left home, he was eager to reassure her of his determination to make this his last mission, and keep his promise that they would be together. And yet, there was no disguising the risks.

'Will you see Heneage?' She asked. 'For you can never trust him to keep his word – whatever Sir Robert Cecil says. Come to that, can you even trust Cecil?'

'I think I can,' he answered… but on a sudden, doubts arose. He knew little of his new spymaster, except that he was most likely as ruthless as any of the Queen's closest councillors. For one night, Revill had been able to forget his situation… now, the enormity of his task fell upon him once again.

'I'll get word to you when I can – if I can,' he said. Then, after throwing the coverlet aside, he rose quickly and began to dress.

Within the hour he was riding back into Lord Ballater's makeshift camp, to find His Lordship's servants up and about already. At his approach they gathered in a body, and at the hostile looks thrown his way, his spirits sank. From being in the arms of his beloved, he was back to being an outsider again.

'I had a mind to let my horse gallop,' he said, in answer to Harman's question as to where he had been. 'He's unused to travelling so slowly... is there anything for breakfast?'

His answer was a surly silence. And thereafter, the silence persisted for most of the day until, to the relief of all, the Queen's Progress arrived at the great mansion of Cowdray. Taut as a bowstring, Revill watched the other men without their noticing. It was the fifteenth day of August... and it would turn out to mark the start of some unexpected events.

***

The stay was to last a week, it transpired, with hunting, dancing, feasting and entertainment: Sir Anthony Browne had spared no expense to play host to his Queen. Hence, those travelling with her vast retinue had time to rest, repair their carts, tend their animals and enjoy the break from travelling. The lords, gentlemen and their ladies took full advantage of their host, roaming the house and its surrounds, wandering the fine gardens or riding to hunt in the park. The servants too had chance to mingle, if only to grumble about their superiors. It was the closest to a holiday they had known in weeks.

Lord Ballater's party, housed in a hastily-converted barn some distance from the house, were relieved at least not to be sleeping in tents. His Lordship had private quarters, curtained off from the rest of the building. Meals were often taken outdoors, provided by the army of cooks the master of Cowdray had hired. Revill, seated on a bench under a tree, was finishing his dinner on the first day after their arrival when a horseman cantered up and hailed him, causing him to look up in surprise.

'So this is where you've been hiding,' Nicholas Godwin said, brightly enough.

A RELUCTANT HERO

'By the Christ,' Revill murmured. 'I thought I'd seen the last of you, back at Farnham.'

'That's not much of a welcome on a hot day,' the other replied. 'Won't you spare me some of what's in that jug?'

With a nod, Revill stood up as Godwin dismounted. There was ale still in the jug, which he poured into his cup and held out. Having quenched his thirst, the Crown Purveyor sat down on the bench and stretched out his legs. After a moment, Revill sat down beside him.

'I recall you saying you were to serve a nobleman in the Queen's train,' Godwin said, without looking at him. 'Though I was surprised to learn it was old Ballater. He's a shameless Papist, and a pauper to boot.'

'I know that,' Revill said... at which, His Lordship's words came to his mind, back at Mistress Bradby's: *what choice does a pauper have?*

'So, you know why he's here, then,' Godwin continued. 'Then, who doesn't?'

'Why do you think he's here?' Revill enquired.

'To seek some relief from his debts, of course,' came the reply. 'Rumour has it he's sold all he has, back in Northamptonshire... the price of recusancy, eh?'

At that Revill fell silent, though it was no surprise: the small number of servants, the air of unease that often seemed to prevail among them... it fitted well enough. Though how Lord Ballater intended to remedy his predicament looked an impossible task. Surely he did not expect an audience with the Queen? Given the unlikelihood of that being granted – let alone it resulting in a favourable conclusion - it still appeared to Revill that the portly old Lord was a most unlikely threat to Elizabeth. And yet, there was a priest in his company; just now, none of it made much sense.

'Which pricks my curiosity a good deal, Perrot,' Godwin said, breaking his thoughts. 'To whit, what in God's name are you doing here?'

'Ex-soldiers can't be too picky, when employment is offered,' Revill said. 'Let's say I needed a change of air.'

'And that's all, is it?' The Crown Purveyor looked unconvinced.

'That's all I'm going to tell you,' Revill answered. 'And now I think on it, why are you here? I didn't know you were part of the Progress.'

The other gave a sigh and, to his relief, changed the topic.

'In truth, I'm at a loose end,' he volunteered. 'There are other Purveyors here now, somewhat more important than myself. Though things might change, when we leave here and head towards Chichester. In the meantime...' He threw Revill a sly look, reminding him of when they shared a chamber in Farnham. 'In the meantime, there's a village called Steadham, barely a mile from here... what say you we slip away tonight, the two of us? Get drunk, and find a couple of trulls? Can't you quit the fat old lord's service for a few hours?'

Somewhat suspiciously, Revill met his eye. 'What, are you so short of company?'

'Well now, what if I am?' Godwin countered. 'You think men in my position are welcomed here with open arms? You said it yourself once, as I recall: we're hated. Or is it merely that you dislike me? As it happens, I don't care for you either – but even so, it's no obstacle to us having some revelry while we can, is it?'

'I suppose not,' Revill answered. In fact, he was tempted. He had had no occasion to relax and drink in convivial company for what already seemed an age... and since missing Tom Bright at his old lodgings, he felt the urge all the more. Moreover, the chance to forsake Harman and the others for a while was not to be missed. He had managed to evade Ballater's party before – why could he not do so again?

'Let's do it, then,' he said. 'I'll drink with you, but I'll forgo seeking a trull.'

'Any particular reason?' Godwin enquired. 'You're not married, are you?'

'Just now,' Revill answered, 'I'm as good as married to Lord Ballater. But tonight, I intend to fly the coop.'

***

The inn was The Woolpack: a low building on the edge of the village, with sagging thatch and grimy windows. On entering, the two of them were unsurprised to find it crowded, villagers heavily outnumbered by men from the Royal Progress who, like them, had escaped their duties for the evening. With every table taken, and even standing room sparse, they ordered mugs of the house ale and found a space close to the wall.

'Where are the women?' Godwin wanted to know, peering through the tobacco smoke.'Surely Steadham boasts a whore or two?'

'Plenty of business for them now, I expect,' Revill said drily. 'Probably worked to the bone.'

'You remember the hostess back at Farnham – the fair Mistress Hickes?' The other asked, with a smirk. 'I bedded her in the end, I swear. That faithful wife act was but a sham, as I thought. Lucky you didn't take my wager, or you'd have lost.'

'I'll take your word for it,' Revill said, not wishing to hear more.

The two of them drank in silence, eying the company. The door opened to admit several more men, some of whom Revill recognised vaguely from the Progress. The sweating drawers, carrying handfuls of mugs back and forth at speed, would soon be exhausted, he thought... when on a sudden Godwin stiffened, as one of the new arrivals caught his eye.

'Someone you know?' Revill enquired.

The other showed unease. 'Just another of my calling,' he muttered.

With mild curiosity, Revill regarded the fellow. Plainly-dressed in black doublet and feathered hat, and wearing a sword, he looked no different to many of the Crown officials who accompanied the sovereign on her travels. With him was another man, unarmed... whereupon, in an instant, it was Revill's turn to give a start.

'Don't tell me you know him too?' Godwin asked.

'No.' Revill was frowning. 'But as it happens, I know his friend... or at least, I think I do.'

At once, his mind flew back almost two years: to the rainy autumn day when he had entered the house in Seething Lane in London. There he had been conducted to a room where he expected to find Sir Francis Walsingham - only to face the Vice-Chamberlain, Sir Thomas Heneage; Revill hadn't known it then, but it was the start of his troubles. Though it was not Heneage he thought of: instead, he recalled the busy little clerk who had shown him in - and had no doubt now that it was him.

And yet, he reasoned, why should it be a surprise? A number of Heneage's servants would be travelling with him, his clerk among them; it was quite likely that, now that the courtiers and councillors were settled at Cowdray, he would have begged an evening to himself. Moreover, the Woolpack, as far as Revill knew, was the only inn for miles. Taking a pull from his mug, he watched the man pick his way through the throng behind his burlier companion, towards the barrels where a drawer was busy working the spigot. While they waited to be served, the two started a conversation. They had not noticed Revill or Godwin.

'So, who's your man?' Godwin asked. 'Old friend, or old enemy?'

'Well, neither,' Revill said. 'But in view of whom he serves, I wonder what he's doing in the company of one of yours. I take it that the one with the sword is a Crown Purveyor, like you?' And when the other nodded: 'Owe him money, do you?'

'If I did, I wouldn't be here talking to you. I'd be lying in a ditch somewhere... or in an alley, with a sore head.'

In spite of everything, Revill was amused. 'He must be a rogue and a half, then,' he said. 'A particularly bad apple among a whole barrel of bad apples, some might say.'

'Mock if you like, Perrot,' his companion retorted. 'You may think me a rogue, but I'm not a hard-hearted bastard like Hooper.'

'Is that his name?' Revill asked. 'Well now, if you don't owe him money, what discomforts you about encountering Master Hooper?'

But when Godwin made no answer he turned to look again – not at Hooper, but at the other one: Heneage's crabbed little clerk, looking ill-at-ease among the noisy crowd. It seemed an odd coupling...

'Oh Christ, he's seen me.'

Revill glanced sharply at Godwin, to see him looking uncomfortable. Whereupon he turned back, grasped the situation in a moment and tensed. The next moment, hemmed in by the throng of customers, he could only stand his ground as the man named Hooper pushed his way determinedly towards them. Beside him, he sensed rather than saw Godwin step back.

'By Jesus, will you look who it is?' The feather-hatted Purveyor said as he came up, in an unmistakeable London accent. 'Old Nick Godwin, the lasses' bane. I must have missed you in Farnham - but no matter, for you're going to buy me and my friend a mug. Get your purse out, and hurry it up!'

With a sneer he turned his gaze upon Revill, whose hand was upon his sword-hilt in an instant.

And even as their eyes met, battle was drawn.

FIVE

At first, it looked as if the matter might have been settled without violence. With a swift glance at Revill, Godwin put a restraining hand out and faced the belligerent Hooper.

'I'll buy you a drink,' he said quickly. 'If I'd known you were coming, I might have-'

'You'd have shat your breeches, sirrah – that's what you'd have done,' the other broke in harshly. 'Remember the Dolphin, by Bishopsgate? I had you by the cods there, didn't I? And bowl me over like a ninepin if I can't do it again!'

A moment passed, then:

'I don't think you will,' Revill put in, thinking he had held his peace for long enough.

'What's that?' Hooper turned deliberately to him, raising his eyebrows in mock amazement. 'Did I hear you speak, sir?'

'You did,' Revill answered. 'Master Godwin and I were having a talk, and I don't recall either of us inviting you. As for treating you to a mug, you look as if you can well afford to buy your own.'

'Perrot, enough!' Godwin tugged at his sleeve. 'There's no cause for wrangling. If I choose to buy the man a drink, I'll-'

'Who said anything about choosing?' Hooper broke in, his neck stiffening like a bullock's. To Revill he said: 'Whoever you are, friend, I'd advise you to step away. This is a private matter between Crown Purveyors – Royal servants. Understand me?'

But to that, Revill merely sighed. 'I think it best we take our business outside, don't you?' He suggested.

'Oh, for Jesus' sake.' Godwin was fumbling for his purse. 'There's no need, damn it.' Hastily, he produced a threepence piece and held it out. 'Take it!'

But Hooper made no move to do so. Keeping his eyes on Revill, he brought his thick-bearded face closer. 'Well now, on reflection I believe I'll accept this man's offer, instead,' he murmured, showing his teeth. 'It's a mite crowded in here, is it not?'

A RELUCTANT HERO

Godwin stiffened, but gave no answer.

'What of your friend?' Revill enquired, with a nod towards the one he had recognised as Heneage's clerk; the man was now peering in their direction. 'Will he come too?'

'He will if I tell him to,' Hooper replied. 'Shall we go?'

And so, a few moments later, the four men stepped out of the door of the Woolpack and walked behind the building onto a grassy space, out of sight of customers. They were an odd group: Revill and Hooper, prepared to fight if need be; Godwin, who looked as if fighting was something he would prefer to avoid... and the black-gowned clerk, who was plainly scared out of his wits.

'What in heaven's name are you doing?' The little man demanded of Hooper. 'If there's to be a brabble, I want no part of it. You, sir...' He turned quickly to Revill. 'You look like a sober man – would you care to explain?'

Somewhat warily, Revill met his eye. It had occurred to him that the clerk might remember him from two years back, even though they had met only briefly, but there was no sign of recognition. Besides, it was growing dark... he gave a shrug.

'Let's say I don't like bullies,' he replied. 'Or even Crown Purveyors, come to that. Which makes we wonder what you're doing in this man's company - sir.'

The clerk, however, was disinclined to answer that. 'What are you attempting?' He demanded of Hooper. 'Think of the consequences – it's akin to madness, I tell you!'

'Close your mouth, Master Bryant,' Hooper snapped. 'And stop quivering, will you? You're not at risk, but you can act as a witness.'

'Witness to what?' Came the anxious reply.

'To the fact – should it come to pass – that I wounded this man in self-defence, of course.' Placing a hand on his sword, the belligerent eyed Revill grimly.

'Stop – cease this, before you regret it!'

It was Godwin who broke in, summoning the courage to step between the two of them. 'This man's a servant to Lord Ballater,' he said to Hooper. 'If you harm him – let alone slay him - you'll pay the heaviest price. Have you forgotten we're on the Verge?'

'But I have witnesses,' Hooper retorted. 'Two of them...' He glared at Godwin. 'You wouldn't accuse me of starting anything, would you?'

A silence fell, in which Godwin and Bryant looked uneasily at each other. Revill wondered what hold Hooper might have over the two of them, but this was no time for speculation. He saw the look in the challenger's eye; he had seen it a hundred times, on fields of battle and elsewhere. Some men just wanted to fight, to prove they mattered in the world.

And the next moment, in the gathering dusk, both combatants stepped away from the other men and drew their rapiers.

It would not last long, Revill decided; he knew that he outmatched his opponent, who was no ex-soldier. He had faced braggarts and rogues before, and had no intention of doing anything more than teaching the man a lesson. When Hooper gave himself away with a sudden tightening of his jaw he was ready, and parried his lunge easily. He then made a rapid sweep to the left, purposefully missing his opponent's ear by a whisker. With a frown Hooper lunged again, but found his blade thrust aside, towards the ground.

'Do you wish to continue?' Revill enquired, in a voice of unconcern. 'There's no shame in a tactical withdrawal.'

'By the Christ!' Angrily, the other took a short step backwards. 'I'll pay you out, you varlet... withdrawal, is it?' And with that, he reached behind and pulled a poniard from his belt.

But when Revill merely drew his own dagger, a look of uncertainty showed on Hooper's face. Breathing harder, he flicked his sword aside in an attempt to distract his opponent, while bringing his left hand up sharply.

Revill stabbed him on the back of the hand, and stood back as blood showed.

With a hiss of pain, Hooper dropped his dagger. But this, Revill well knew, could precipitate the most dangerous part of the bout: in pain and fury, a man might become reckless. Sure enough, Hooper gave a wild cry and lurched forward, wielding his sword with his right hand. There came a cry of alarm from nearby – Revill believed it was from Bryant – as the combatants engaged…

Until, quite quickly, it was over.

Knocking Hooper's blade aside, Revill allowed the hilt of his rapier to lock with his, letting the other think he was putting all his strength into the move. But as they grappled, he brought his poniard up swiftly and put its point to the great artery in his neck. At the sudden prick of cold metal, the man went rigid.

'Lower your weapon and cast it aside,' Revill breathed.

A moment, a muffled curse… then Hooper went limp and dropped the sword. And at Revill's next order, he fell to his knees. There was a gasp of relief from behind, and Godwin appeared, his face pale in the gathering gloom.

'Good God.' He peered down at his fellow Purveyor, who was scowling at the ground. 'I thought you-'

'What, that I would put an end to him?' Revill said, without looking up from his victim. 'You said yourself, we're on the Verge. I've no wish to be hanged on account of this one.'

'Thank the Lord for that,' came another voice. Master Bryant came forward, his eyes on Revill. 'You did right, sir,' he added. 'This… this disagreement should go no further. It's in no man's interest to speak of it… do you concur?'

He was addressing Hooper, who now looked up balefully.

'Concur?' he echoed. 'I say to the devil with you – and with him!' With a wild look at Revill, who kept the poniard's point to his throat, he added. 'You may have won this hand, but the game isn't over. You may stake everything on it!'

'I don't gamble,' Revill said, though it hadn't always been true. 'But your companion here talks sense… Master Bryant?' He glanced briefly at the clerk.

'I'll tend his wound myself,' Bryant said, nodding quickly. 'A cut, nothing more… shall we return to Cowdray?'

That question too was for Hooper, who made no answer. But seeing the crisis had passed, Revill removed his dagger and sheathed it, then thrust his sword back in the scabbard. Slowly, the loser of the bout got to his feet.

'I want a drink,' he muttered. 'And I'm going back to the inn.' He picked up his sword and sheathed it. Then, tugging a kerchief from his sleeve, he began wrapping it about his injured hand. 'Are you coming?'

He was addressing Godwin, who hesitated. In surprise, Revill met his eye.

'It's naught… a bit of old business,' Godwin told him, somewhat guardedly. 'Besides, I didn't ask you to intervene.' Lowering his gaze, he followed Hooper, who was already walking away. Soon both had rounded the corner of the inn, leaving Revill and Bryant alone.

'I'll be gone now,' the little clerk said, glancing about… whereupon, on nothing more than impulse, Revill stepped close to him.

'Won't you spare me a moment first?' he asked.

Bryant flinched. 'Why?'

'You're one of Sir Thomas Heneage's company, are you not?'

'I am his secretary,' came the swift reply. 'And I intend to return to him now… I've had enough excitement for one night.'

'So have I, but I confess my curiosity is aroused,' Revill said. 'To whit, what would Sir Thomas's secretary be doing in the company of a roguish Purveyor like Master Hooper?'

'That's none of your affair,' Bryant answered. 'Now, if you'll pardon me…'

He was turning to leave, when to his alarm Revill placed a hand on his shoulder. 'There's no hurry, is there?' He murmured. 'After all, I saved you from having to stand witness in what could have been a most tiresome enquiry. Will you not stay a while?'

The little man blinked, looked up at Revill… and gave a start.

'By heaven, I've seen you before,' he said with a frown. 'In London, was it not? Though your name means nothing… Perrot, is it?'

'It is,' Revill replied. 'And as Godwin said, I guard Lord Ballater. Yet I'd be interested to hear of your business with Hooper. Knowing what I do of men like him - and Godwin too - I might even suspect you of some kind of double dealing…am I close?'

A RELUCTANT HERO

He paused, noticing beads of sweat on the other's brow. It was a warm night, but…

'I have no idea what you mean,' Bryant retorted. 'But you're unwise, threatening a man like me. One word to my master, and you'd be-'

'Threatening?' Revill echoed. 'Why, a pox on the very thought. I merely…'

He stopped himself; a plan had just flown to his mind that might prove useful - that might even, he realised, be an answer to his difficulties with Heneage. It was a wild notion, but:

'I merely thought the two of us might do business, between ourselves,' he went on. 'I too have connections, you might say.'

But his answer, when it came, was most indignant.

'Perhaps you didn't hear me,' Bryant said, summoning what dignity he could. 'But let me speak plainly: I have no notion what it is what you refer to, nor do I have any desire to deal with a man like you. As for connections…' a suggestion of a smirk appeared. 'I think you'll find the influence of an impoverished Papist like Lord Ballater, would count for little against that of Her Majesty's Vice-Chamberlain.'

'How does it work, then?' Revill asked, looking unconcerned. 'Hooper underpays for purchases he makes during the Progress – orders signed by the Vice-Chamberlain himself, perhaps – then inflates the bills, and the two of you split the difference? Perhaps you even forge Heneage's signature… not too difficult for someone in your position, eh?'

This time the effect was instantaneous: the little clerk drew a sharp breath and stepped back. For his part, Revill gave a low whistle of admiration, and shook his head. 'Ingenious – not to say courageous,' he murmured, seizing his advantage. 'Given the quantity of provisions the Queens' train consumes over these weeks of travel - grain, livestock, and all the rest – we could be speaking of a goodly sum of money here, could we not? Why, I believe I've misjudged you, Master Bryant. You're a deal cleverer than you look.'

The little clerk swallowed, and lowered his head. 'You can't prove any of this,' he mumbled. 'And I don't-'

'Come now, be of good cheer,' Revill broke in, surprised that it had been so easy. 'We have more in common than you think. I too serve a master I dislike. More, I've a fair idea of what our friend Godwin gets up to. Can't you and I fashion something, together?'

'I can't... I pray you, don't trouble me further,' Bryant said quickly; he appeared genuinely alarmed now. 'You walk a dangerous path, if you do. Now let me leave, and let us forget we ever met, shall we?'

'No-one's stopping you leaving,' Revill said. 'But as for forgetting we met...' he shook his head. 'It would be hard to avoid each other, once the Progress moves on again, would it not?

Briefly the little clerk met his eye, before turning and hurrying off. Revill stood still, musing on what had occurred: a matter of only minutes, but minutes that could prove important.

For a moment he considered returning to the inn, then dismissed the notion. Instead he started back on the road to Cowdray, his mind busy. He had the feeling that, in view of what Sir Thomas Heneage's secretary had unwittingly revealed, he had just acquired a weapon: something he might even use against his old nemesis.

***

The Queen had spent some days at Cowdray, when a change occurred in Lord Ballater's party that drove other matters from Revill's mind. One afternoon, having occupied himself exercising Malachi, he noticed that Dickon was missing. Then he realised that he had seen nothing of the young man for a while. Encountering Harman outside the barn, he raised the matter casually.

'He's left my master's service,' the steward said gruffly.

'Why is that?' Revill enquired. 'I thought he was devoted to His Lordship.'

'He is, as are we all - save you,' Harman growled. 'And it's naught to you what he does.'

He was about to move away, but Revill sensed something: under his habitual bluster, the man was uneasy. Stepping closer, he spoke low. 'He's not been dismissed, then?'

'Of course he hasn't!' The steward glared at him. 'Now leave me be!'

A RELUCTANT HERO

Revill watched him stalk off, then turned away. He had a mind to take a walk around the grounds and think things over; of late the urgency of his assignment from Cecil, to discover a potential assassin in Ballater's company, had been somewhat dulled, he thought. Thus far, the stay at Cowdray had passed peacefully – indeed, it had been a great success for Sir Anthony Browne, and the Queen was said to be well pleased. In a few days' time the Progress would move off southwards, to a place called West Dean; the danger to Her Majesty, which Revill had feared, now looked almost like a chimera. Lord Ballater himself was of good cheer, and seemed to have mingled affably enough with other noblemen. Though Revill had a good idea where he was, most of the time: he even suspected that a mass might have been held once, somewhere in the great house, while the Queen and her followers were being entertained in the main hall. It would mean there was indeed a priest in residence, hidden in one of the ingeniously-devised hiding holes that everyone knew about, but few had ever seen… at which notion, Revill stopped walking.

Dickon… the priest in disguise. Had he simply left Ballater's train, to take up residence here? Indeed, could this have been his intention all along – and was His Lordship aware of it?

The notion astounded him. Under the eyes of the Queen and her Councillors, the mild-mannered young man might have passed into the service of one of the most prominent Catholics without even being noticed. Which meant that His Lordship's train would be reduced merely to Harman, Hawkins and himself: barely enough to carry out the tasks required… would that not cause some raised eyebrows?

He was still musing on the matter that evening at supper, when the answer to that question came with the arrival of a new man: one who, it transpired, was to join Ballater's company as a replacement for Dickon.

His name was John Shearer; and the moment he saw him, Revill's suspicions rose at once.

***

Master Shearer, it seemed, was a man of good family, whose home was not too far distant. He had been recommended to Lord

Ballater - by an acquaintance, it seemed - as a capable fellow, who could fulfil any tasks Dickon had previously performed. But he was no scholar, and certainly no priest-in-disguise. The moment he and Revill set eyes on each other, each recognised the other as a fighting man, who would shrink from no-one.

'I'm told you serve as His Lordship's bodyguard, Master Perrot,' the newcomer said, when the men sat down to eat. 'A former soldier, then?'

'I was once,' Revill allowed.

To that, Hawkins gave a snort that conveyed his contempt; since the day they had met, he had barely spoken to Revill. Harman quaffed beer from his tankard, and said nothing.

Shearer went quiet for a while, busying himself at his roast mutton. Revill saw a stocky, black-haired and black-bearded man in good clothes. His horse he had already admired, as one who would match Malachi for breeding and stamina. By way of conversation, he asked whether Shearer had been active on the Queen's service, only to receive a shrug.

'No war service,' the man replied. 'Unless you count guarding the docks at Portsmouth as such. Tedious work, is that.'

'Important work, though,' Revill said. 'There's always danger from across the Channel, is there not?'

'Well, that's true,' Shearer agreed. 'Some say the Queen decided to come south chiefly to view the state of the nation's defences. Then again, perhaps she simply hopes for news of the Earl of Essex, over in France. Always tardy with his reports is Essex, from what I've heard.' And when Harman glanced up with a frown, he added: 'Soldiers' gossip, master steward. The men I serve with have little occasion to do much else.'

'I've no time for it, myself,' Harman said, with a forbidding look. 'Prefer to keep busy. The word is we'll be leaving in a couple of days. Her Majesty wants to be at West Dean for the Sabbath, which means we'll have plenty to do. No more sloping off to drink in taverns, as I hear a good number of her servants have done.'

He threw a glance at Revill, who ignored him and kept his attention on Shearer.

A RELUCTANT HERO

'It's a fine horse you have,' he said. 'Perhaps we'll ride together, along the way.'

'Perhaps,' the new man replied, without expression.

Hawkins gave another snort, and glowered at his platter.

No more was said after that. But on the following afternoon, when the party were packing in preparation to move, Revill received a message that both alerted and intrigued him. He was carrying spare horse-harness to the cart, when a boy appeared from the direction of the great house and asked if he was Master Perrot. On receiving an answer, he held out a paper rolled into a tight tube.

'For me?' Revill said. 'Who is it from?'

But the boy, one of the kitchen servants, merely shook his head. Revill dumped the harness on the wagon, took the missive and reached for his purse.

'A halfpenny for your pains,' he said, proffering the coin. The messenger accepted it, then hurried off before Revill could address him again. Glancing about to see that no-one was near, he unrolled the paper and read.

It was from Thomas Bryant, Heneage's secretary, asking Revill to meet with him alone after dark on the far side of the paddock. There were no further details, save a brief sentence to the effect that it would be greatly to his advantage.

Revill lowered the letter… and immediately smelled a trap.

This request, he suspected, had Hooper's stamp on it. Bryant would almost certainly have told him of their conversation behind the inn, after his departure. Hence, Revill knew he could be seen as a threat to whatever dealings the two of them were involved in. With a frown, he thought then of Godwin… could he be a party to this, too?

He stowed the message in his doublet and walked back to the barn. When darkness came, he would of course keep the appointment. He would have liked to take a companion with him too, but there was no-one.

He was an outsider still, and must look to his own self-preservation.

SIX

Night-time came slowly, on their last day at Cowdray. The Queen's servants had been busy from morning until twilight, fetching and carrying. Carts were loaded and covered, tents struck, and several hundred people had gone to their beds in readiness for an early start on the morrow.

Meanwhile Will Revill, lying in his blanket on a straw-filled pallet, feigned slumber until he was satisfied that all of his fellows slept soundly.

At last, judging the moment, he arose in silence, padded to the barn door carrying his shoes, then slipped outside into the balmy night. There was moonlight, which was a blessing, though now and again a cloud drifted across. Stepping away from the building, he retrieved his sword from the bushes where he had hidden it before retiring, on account of the noise he might have made; fortunately, no-one seemed to have noticed its absence. Dressed and alert, he then walked towards the broad paddock where many of the horses were corralled, Malachi among them. On a corner post a lantern burned, but there were no guards; hereabouts, Sir Anthony Browne's name was enough to ensure their safety.

On reaching the fence, he paused. From the house, lights still showed; likely the Queen, known for enjoying late nights on her Progresses, was keeping company. Here in the paddock horses snickered and stamped, sensing his presence. Silently he moved forward, skirting the fence until the soft thud of approaching hooves made him start... but it was only Malachi. The old warhorse knew his master's scent and came trotting up, tossing his head.

'No exercise until tomorrow,' Revill murmured, reaching across the rail to pat his neck. 'Now rest - and wish me good fortune.'

A moment later he had left the paddock and stepped into the fringe of trees that loomed behind. He grasped his sword hilt, checking that it was loose in the scabbard. Then he put a hand

A RELUCTANT HERO

inside his doublet and felt for the wheel-lock pistol that he had secreted. It was not loaded, but its presence was reassuring. Apart from the poniard at his back, he carried no other means of defence - apart from his luck.

The wood closed about him, in eerie silence. Somewhere a nightbird called, but otherwise there was barely a rustle of leaves. He walked further, almost to where the trees began to thin again. Finally he stopped, breathed in and announced himself.

'Are you there, Bryant? It's Perrot.'

There was no answer. He waited, looking about in the gloom, wondering whether he should have taken the lantern from its post; as it was, if more than one person came at him out of the dark, he would be hard-pressed to respond...

A sudden noise startled him, closer than he liked; it could have been the snap of a twig, or nothing more than a rabbit bounding away. Turning swiftly, he peered through the trees but saw nothing. Hand on sword he listened – until at last came a voice he recognised.

'I'm here... I'm alone, so be at ease.'

Revill watched, alert for the least indication of trickery, until a shape appeared from behind a tree. Gingerly the figure approached, lifting his arms to show he carried no weapon. Finally Bryant, clad in his gown, stood before him.

'I wasn't sure you would come,' the little clerk said, somewhat hastily. 'After what I said to you back at the Woolpack, I mean. Now I've... well, I've reconsidered, shall I say.'

'Have you, indeed?' Revill took a step forward, close enough to threaten him. But the man was harmless - assuming that he was truly alone. Revill still found that hard to believe.

'Yes... in view of your offer,' Bryant went on. 'We might, perhaps, come to something after all... an arrangement? Given your obvious qualities, that is. Courage and prudence, not to mention restraint, do not always reside together in a man, I've found.'

'I'm flattered,' Revill said, sensing that this was flattery with a purpose. Some distance away he could see the lantern, dimly flickering on the paddock fence... shifting his gaze back to Bryant, he waited.

'The matter is, it's not quite what you think,' Heneage's secretary said. He swallowed, loud enough for Revill to hear him.

'It's not?'

'No, and you shouldn't rush to judgement. I'm a loyal servant to the Vice-Chamberlain – I would never put my position in jeopardy. And as for forging his signature...' the man almost shuddered. 'The very thought appals me. You were harsh in your accusations, Perrot.'

Now that his eyes had grown accustomed to the near-darkness, Revill was able to look him over. He saw nervousness, which was perhaps to be expected, but nothing worse.

'Given your association with a man like Hooper, I felt inclined to be harsh,' Revill said. 'But I doubt you're here for an apology. Your letter spoke of an advantage to me.'

'Indeed... I will speak of it soon,' Bryant said. But he hesitated, and Revill's suspicions arose again; the man seemed merely to be playing for time.

'Why not do so now?' He invited. 'Or were you waiting for someone else?'

'Of course not. I said I was alone, did I not? And I've taken a considerable risk to meet with you like this, so...'

But he trailed off, and now Revill saw it: Bryant was babbling. It was a trap - what else would it be? For a moment, he considered drawing out his pistol and putting the fear of God into him, until a sound from behind made him whirl about...

Too late.

There was a blinding flash, a thunderous report, and something thudded into his chest: a hammer blow that sent him sprawling onto his back. Winded and dazed, he glimpsed a figure coming forward to stand over him... then voices.

'By heaven, why did you delay?' It was Bryant. 'A moment longer, and he would have-'

'Stop your wheedling!' The other, whoever he was, cut him off swiftly. He was peering down at Revill - who realised on a sudden

A RELUCTANT HERO

that he was not bleeding. More, if he had been shot in the chest, he ought to be dead... he held his breath, and kept his eyes closed.

'I'm leaving,' Bryant said then, his voice shaking. 'I've done my part!'

'You'll wait,' came the sharp response. 'First, I need to make sure.'

Taut from head to foot, with heart racing and a throbbing pain under his ribs, Revill sensed that his assailant was bending over him. Then came the scratch of a flint, as a flame was kindled. Soon the man would realise that, by some miracle, the shot had not proved fatal...

Then it dawned on him what had occurred - and it was indeed a miracle, of a sort. The ball had slammed into the stock of Revill's pistol, inside his coat. Now he knew why he wasn't spurting blood. But the relief was short-lived, to be replaced by the realisation that the truth was about to be discovered. He heard a sword being drawn, and tensed himself to roll away...

Whereupon several more things happened, in quick succession.

First came footfalls, rapid and heavy, drawing close. Then a cry of alarm, which could only have come from Bryant. A shout followed, then a screech of pain, and the noise of someone crashing to earth. A flurry of movement, another cry... and Revill opened his eyes, to blink at the tableau that played before him.

Close by, a tinder-box lay sputtering on the ground, its flame waning rapidly. But there was enough time to see a figure lying flat, with another standing over it. Meanwhile Bryant hopped about in terror, as if uncertain which way to run. The standing figure held a dagger; Revill saw it gleam briefly before the flame went out, plunging all into semi-darkness again. But he heard a choking sound from the man on the ground... then a sigh, and silence.

Sitting up painfully, he peered at the person who had just saved his life. Hearing movement, that one turned sharply, stepped towards him and revealed himself: John Shearer.

'By God.' Revill gazed upwards. 'What are you-'

He broke off, looking aside as movement caught his eye: Master Bryant, it seemed, had decided to make his escape. But as he darted off in the direction of the paddock, Shearer was quicker. Covering the yards that separated them he lurched, seized the little clerk by an arm and threw him against the trunk of a tree. With a yelp, Bryant fell on his rump.

'Stay there,' Shearer ordered. 'Or I'll be obliged to use this again.' He held up his dagger, which caused the other to whimper.

Slowly, Revill got to his feet. 'I don't know why you're here, but I'm mighty glad of it,' he murmured.

'Are you hurt?' Shearer stepped closer. 'When he shot you, I thought that was the end.'

'It would have been,' Revill replied, breathing steadily.' Had I not been carrying this.' He began to unbutton his doublet, stiffening at the pain in his chest. There was some blood after all, he realised... a trickle, soaking through his shirt.

'I'll make light.' Shearer stepped away, bent and retrieved the tinder box that Revill's assailant had dropped. After some fumbling and a striking of flint, a new flame appeared. Meanwhile Revill tugged his arms free and dropped his doublet, allowing his pistol to fall to the ground. Then, as Shearer brought the light near, they examined the wound together.

The ball, it was revealed, had shattered the butt of Revill's wheel-lock, driving splinters of oak into his flesh. And yet, the weapon had saved his life.

'You're a lucky man,' Shearer said. 'And a bold one too, I might add. What possessed you to come out here alone?'

'In truth, very little.' Recovering himself, Revill glanced at Bryant, sitting rigid with his back to the tree. 'I had some words with that man at an inn, two nights ago. I was curious...'

But at the look on the other's face, he broke off: he hadn't believed a word of it. And when Shearer stepped closer – too close for comfort – the reason for his timely arrival was out.

'I was told you're a reckless man, at times – Master Perrot,' he said, speaking so low that no-one else could have heard. And when Revill frowned, he added: 'That's why Sir Robert Cecil told me to watch your back. He was right, was he not?'

A RELUCTANT HERO

Revill met his gaze, and let out a breath. 'I suppose he was,' he admitted. 'So, should I ask who you are? Or do we remain servants to Lord Ballater, who know nothing of each other?'

'We'll have to, for the present,' came the reply. 'But just now we've matters to attend to, have we not?'

'Indeed we have.' Revill looked round at Bryant. 'Like how to deal with our friend there.'

'He can help us, can't he?'

Shearer walked over to the little clerk and ordered him to get up. When he did so, clearly in fear for his life, he gripped his arm and steered him towards the body of Revill's assailant. Revill followed, and found himself looking down at a stranger: a heavy-browed man-at-arms, his jerkin soaked with blood as a result of the death-blow Shearer had administered.

'Who was he?' Shearer enquired, letting go of Bryant.

The other gulped. 'One of Heneage's men... a ruffian. I had naught to do with him.'

Revill eyed him. 'But, do you think you can account for his absence?'

'Me?' Shakily, Bryant looked up. 'I don't know... what do you intend to do?'

'Conceal the body,' Shearer told him. 'Tomorrow, the Queen's Progress moves on. It will be some time before anyone stumbles upon a dead man in the wood. By then, the foxes and crows will likely have rendered him difficult to identify.'

'Good God.' Bryant swallowed. 'I beg you, let me go now,' he said, wetting his lips. 'I'll not say a word about this, I swear... and perhaps I can contrive a tale, about this man leaving in the night. Shall I do that?'

He looked at Revill, nodding eagerly. A moment passed, before Revill turned to Shearer.

'We'll do as you suggest,' he said. 'Then you should go back. But leave this one to me.'

He indicated Bryant, who gave a start. 'What... what do you mean?' He jabbered. 'I've agreed to help, have I not? You wouldn't-'

'Start gathering up twigs and branches,' Shearer ordered curtly. 'Once we're done, I'm away. I think Master Perrot would like a few words with you after that.'

The little clerk flinched, then hurried to obey.

The work was done quickly. In some pain, Revill stripped to the waist, sat on the ground and by the feeble light of the tinder-box drew the splinters from his flesh as best he could. There were bruises and grazes, but nothing worse. He fashioned a rough bandage from his shirt, tied it about his body and put on his doublet. Meanwhile, aided by a willing Bryant, Shearer covered the corpse with a carpet of foliage until all that could be seen was a slight mound. The man's weapons he buried, using his own dagger to dig a pit; Revill's shattered pistol followed, to be covered with earth and grass. Finally, dusting his hands against his breeches, the one Cecil had sent to keep a watch on Revill stepped away, drawing him aside.

'Don't take too long,' he advised. 'Ballater's people might have noticed our absence. I'll tell them I went out to relieve myself. You?'

'I'll think of something,' Revill replied. 'Meanwhile, you have my heartfelt thanks.'

With a nod, Shearer turned aside and looked to Bryant, who was wiping his hands on his gown and looking nervously in their direction. Then he was gone, disappearing swiftly into the gloom. As his footfalls faded Revill approached the little clerk, who a short time ago had sought to contrive his death. At once, the man shrank away.

'Be at ease,' Revill said. 'That was your advice to me, was it not? What did you think I was about to do, cut you to pieces?' But when the other made no reply, he let out a sigh. 'I want answers,' he said. 'Nothing more. Then, if I'm satisfied, we'll go our ways. You promised to fashion a tale for Heneage, so I'll leave the details to you.'

Whereupon he ordered Bryant to take a sitting position, squatted before him, and invited him to speak. And quite soon, what was revealed began to intrigue him... rather more, in the end, than he could have imagined.

A RELUCTANT HERO

***

He had assumed it was Hooper, the leading Crown Purveyor, who had wanted him dead; whether Godwin had wished it too he was uncertain. In fact, he now learned, neither of them had ordered the ambush.

It was Sir Thomas Heneage.

'I told you before, you walk a dangerous path,' Bryant said, without meeting Revill's eye. 'In truth, you do so still. My master can be-'

'Brutal, as well as treacherous,' Revill finished, looking hard at him. 'I already know that. Now tell me something new, or I might prove somewhat treacherous myself.'

It was an empty threat; Revill was no cold-blooded murderer, but Bryant didn't know that. After what had happened, he was just a frightened lackey, one who had been obliged to step far outside his normal duties. For Heneage needed secrecy: Revill had learned of his corrupt dealings two years before, in the matter of his attempts to force the sale of a property in Surrey and split the proceeds. Now, it was clear to him that Hooper and Godwin, those villainous Purveyors, were not in charge of the faking of monies spent on Crown purchases: their master was Heneage, the Vice-Chamberlain in partial control of the Royal purse-strings.

In spite of what he knew of the man, the boldness of the scheme sobered him. Right under the Queen's nose one of her Privy Councillors was bleeding her coffers, a little at a time: not enough to draw attention, but enough to accrue a tidy sum. How long the practice had been going on, he did not know.

But he could ask Bryant who, it appeared, was willing to tell him almost anything.

'Years, it's been,' the little man said, looking quite miserable now. 'At first, I was afraid to have any part in it, but in the end I had no choice. He cannot be denied… my master, that is. And once Hooper was hired to run things, I was in fear of my life. You've seen how he is – you faced him yourself.'

'What of Godwin?' Revill asked, after a pause. 'Did Hooper threaten him too?'

'I know not,' came the reply. 'Likely he didn't need to. Godwin isn't such a rogue as he, but he's greedy. A weakness for good food and wine... and women.'

For a while Revill took in the words, while the other shivered; it was long past midnight, and the air had cooled. Finally he got stiffly to his feet, and bade the other rise.

'Can I go now?' Bryant asked. 'I've told you enough, have I not?'

'In truth, I'm uncertain,' Revill said. 'I might need to call on your services again.'

At that, the other's face fell. 'In God's name, I pray you will not,' he muttered. 'If my master got an inkling of what I'd told you, my life wouldn't be worth a candle. As it is, he'll know that his orders weren't obeyed, the moment he catches sight of you.'

'I said I'll leave you to explain that,' Revill replied. 'I've spared your life, and that's all I'm about to do.'

He stood aside and waited. Bryant turned to go... then gave a start.

'By the Lord, I knew I'd seen you,' he exclaimed. 'You came to Seething Lane to attend my master... you were captain of a trained-band. You're Revill!'

'Not any more,' Revill said, leaning forward so suddenly that the other blinked. 'My name's Perrot, and I serve Lord Ballater. Do we understand each other?' Upon which, since this was a moment to convince, he drew his dagger swiftly and held it up.

His victim gulped. 'Very well... you may trust me, I swear.'

'I don't, whether you swear or not,' Revill said. 'But I'll have to live with it.'

And so, they parted. Revill watched the man hurry away, his head bowed. After waiting for a short while he followed, making his way back to the barn. The place was in silence when he slipped through the door, shoeless as he had left. He listened, before satisfying himself that no-one was awake... apart from Shearer, he knew.

Thereafter, wrapped in his blanket, Revill stretched out, closed his eyes and waited for the dawn. After his escapade in the wood,

A RELUCTANT HERO

which had brought him closer to losing his life than he had been in a long time, he knew sleep was likely impossible.

***

Morning arrived with distant noises: shouts of drovers, and the general hubbub which always preceded the departure of Her Majesty's Progress. Having dozed briefly despite his hurts, Revill awoke to the sound of Harman stamping into his boots by the open door. Sunlight came in, along with the scent of wood smoke. Hawkins and Shearer, it seemed, were already up and gone from the barn.

'Awake at last?' Harman turned to him sourly. 'Best shake a leg, hadn't you?'

Revill hesitated, remembering that his appearance would draw attention. Fortunately, Harman went out, leaving him alone. Thereafter he lost no time in removing his bandage, to find that there was no fresh bleeding from the lacerations, only a large bruise. Moving quickly, he took a spare shirt from his pack and put it on; the bandage he would dispose of in the bushes. Then he rose and finished dressing... just in time to hear a bellow from the closed-off quarters of Lord Ballater.

'Where is everybody?' His Lordship cried. 'I demand to be served!'

With a sigh, Revill stepped across the barn, drew aside the curtain and made his bow.

The departure was sluggish that day, almost as if nobody wanted to leave; the stay at Cowdray had been a pleasant and peaceful sojourn for everyone – apart from Revill and Shearer, and Sir Thomas Heneage's secretary. And an unfortunate man-at-arms, now lying under a layer of twigs and branches in the wood.

Sobered by the experience, Revill went about his duties in silence; when he and Shearer encountered each other they barely nodded. Soon, when he had saddled Malachi and was ready to mount, he forced himself to focus once more on his mission, which had been somewhat over-shadowed by events. Yet the danger to the Queen, which he had feared might arise at Cowdray, had passed. Sir Anthony Browne had proved a loyal and assiduous host, and the great cavalcade was leaving 'Little Rome' in good spirits. Finally, after warm speeches of thanks and similar speeches of farewell, the train got under way, creaking southwards along the western slopes of the South Downs, to the hamlet of West Dean. Lord Ballater's company as usual brought up the rear, just head of the ox-carts.

Riding close to His Lordship, with Harman and Shearer behind and Hawkins driving the cart, Revill must have appeared grim-faced. He realised it when His Lordship, his immense bulk overflowing the saddle, slowed his horse and addressed him.

'Why so glum, Perrot?' He barked. 'Did life at Cowdray not suit you?'

'It suited me well, my Lord,' Revill replied. 'We wanted for nothing... I trust you enjoyed the entertainment?'

'Entertainment?' Ballater gave a snort. 'It's all one to me. My dancing days are over... I leave that to the prancing popinjays of the Court. In truth, I...'

Abruptly he stopped, caught his breath, then let out a great cough. Revill frowned as the coughing continued, a phlegmatic rasping. Tugging a kerchief from his sleeve, His Lordship put it to his mouth until the fit passed. He was sweating a good deal. Dabbing at his brow, he uttered a low curse that Revill barely heard.

'Are you out of sorts, my Lord?' He enquired. 'Something to drink, or-'

'I'm perfectly well!' Ballater turned sharply. 'You're not my body-servant, are you? Remember your place!'

Briefly Revill met his eye, before slowing Malachi and allowing His Lordship to draw a few paces ahead. But when he chanced to look behind, he found another gaze upon him.

Harman had thrown him a look of more than mere disapproval: it conveyed a warning. Thenceforth he was careful to keep his eyes on the road, and speak to no-one.

But his mind was running over Ballater's demeanour, from the moment he had set eyes on him at Mistress Bradby's house, more than a week ago. And a conclusion arose, that he believed he might have reached sooner.

Lord Ballater was sick, and Harman knew it.

A RELUCTANT HERO

SEVEN

The journey to West Dean, of little more than eight miles, passed without incident. By evening the cavalcade had reached its stopping place: a manor house partly hidden by rows of trees. The place was not as large as Cowdray, and Ballater's party were to be under sailcloth again, which put His Lordship in a poor humour. While the tents were being erected in a nearby meadow he went off to dine with others, leaving orders for his bed to be made ready, for he would retire early. But while his men busied themselves, Revill found a brief moment to speak with Shearer alone. Swiftly he gave an account of his interrogation of Bryant, which caused the other to frown.

'So, what do you propose to do?'

'Can you get a message to Cecil?' Revill asked.

'It's possible,' came the uncertain reply. 'But I'm supposed to keep clear of him. I'm deniable – as you are, I suppose.'

'Even when it's as important as this?'

'Well, I can but try.'

'Do you know anything about the man you replaced?' Revill asked then, on impulse. 'The one who left us at Cowdray?'

Shearer shook his head, whereupon Revill told him of Dickon, his discovery of the man's true role, and the belief that he had gone into service with Sir Anthony Browne. He also mentioned the fact that no-one in Ballater's party had mentioned his absence.

'You mean, they must have known?' And when Revill merely shrugged: 'Well then, mayhap I should try harder to see Cecil.' Seeing Harman approaching, Shearer turned away. Revill too started to move, but the steward stayed him.

'I thought you and I should have a word,' he said, beckoning.

Without expression, Revill moved to join him.

'Where did you go, in the night?' Harman asked abruptly. 'I saw you sneak in.'

'I didn't sneak,' Revill replied. 'I didn't want to wake anyone. Needed some air, that's all.'

'Like Shearer?' The steward assumed one of his belligerent looks. 'I saw him come in, too.'

'I can't speak for Shearer,' Revill said. 'I went walking... I'm a countryman at heart.'

'Are you indeed?' The other peered at him. 'You see, at times I find it hard to believe anything you say... Perrot.'

Revill said nothing.

'As for guarding His Lordship...' Harman gave a snort. 'I haven't seen you do much of that, apart from ride close to him.'

'I keep my eyes open,' Revill told him. He was reminded now of Ballater's words, when they had first met: *My steward thinks you may be a spy*.

'Very wise,' Harman grunted. 'For make no mistake, I'll be keeping my eyes on you.'

Whereupon, with a final glare, he walked off. Revill turned and caught sight of Shearer some distance away, looking in his direction. He gave a nod, then began to busy himself.

And later that day, when His Lordship had gone over to the manor, Shearer was able to pass by Revill and deliver a short verbal message: he was to meet with Cecil at sunset, in the manor house's great kitchen.

'And he's none too pleased,' Shearer murmured.

Revill drew a breath, and set himself to wait for evening.

***

It was a curious location for a meeting, he had thought; but on arrival at the boiling hot kitchen filled with steam and the smell of cooked meats, with shouting cooks and scurrying servants, he understood. Everyone was too busy to pay attention, even when a man as distinguished as Sir Robert Cecil dropped in, seemingly to escape his duties for a moment and take a mug of beer in a corner. Here Revill found the little hunchback, seated beside a table piled with dishes. When Cecil pointed to a nearby beer-keg, he brought it over and sat down amid the bustle.

A RELUCTANT HERO

'You've obliged me to be indiscreet,' were Cecil's first words. 'But since I'm appraised of the importance of the matter, I've broken one of my own rules.'

Revill managed a nod. The man facing him looked tired, he thought, and under some strain; then, the Queen was a demanding woman.

'Shearer says you've something to tell me,' Cecil said, speaking low. Lifting his mug, he took a sip and waited.

So, Revill told him what he had learned. He spoke of Godwin and Hooper, and finally of Bryant. The other listened without expression until he had finished his account - whereupon to Revill's surprise, a trace of a smile appeared.

'What a murky business,' Cecil murmured. 'And what an interrogator you are, I might add. Somehow, I never thought of you as such.'

Revill blinked.

'Yet, I cannot help but think you've strayed somewhat from your purpose,' the little spymaster went on. 'Need I remind you of what that is?'

'I stay close to Lord Ballater whenever I can, sir,' Revill said. 'I've seen naught to be concerned about – until now.' He then spoke of Dickon, and of the man's subsequent disappearance at Cowdray. The response, however, was a surprise.

'I know about him,' Cecil said shortly. 'Your conclusions are correct, but he's not a threat. No more than are a hundred others like him, that is.' He paused, then: 'He's Ballater's son, did you know that?'

'I didn't,' Revill answered, with a frown. 'But now that you've told me-'

'I've told you nothing.'

Having cut him off, Cecil met his gaze: those sharp, falcon-like eyes peering into his. 'I didn't expect to have cause to remind you of your obligations – Perrot,' he added, speaking rapidly. 'That's the name you go under now, I understand? But the first one that comes to mind, is to instruct you to refrain from going off to drink in country inns – let alone getting into brawls. What in God's name were you thinking of?'

'It won't happen again,' Revill said.

'I'm pleased to hear it. Nor, I will say, should you go looking for new conspiracies – isn't one assignment enough?' Cecil paused, then: 'In view of how matters stand, you need to keep an even closer watch on Ballater's servants.' A dry look appeared. 'Though how His Lordship hasn't realised that two of his men are in fact working for me, I can't imagine. Unless he's really as dull-witted as people say. I always found that unlikely.'

He fell silent and took another drink. Revill, sweating in the heat of the kitchen, glanced at his mug, whereupon to his surprise Cecil pushed it towards him.

'Finish that,' he said. 'You've made your report, and I'll return to Her Majesty. But understand this: we shouldn't meet again. If there's anything you think is significant, you can tell Shearer. Meanwhile, tonight you merely sloped away from Ballater's train to beg a mug of beer from the kitchens, where you drank alone. Is that clear?'

'Of course, sir.' Revill nodded, whereupon the other slipped from his stool to the floor, turned and made his way through the throng of kitchen folk. Nobody appeared to notice.

And a short time later, having drained the mug, Revill was walking through the manor grounds, and thence to the tent. Here he found the rest of Lord Ballater's servants, seated and playing at cards. Only Shearer glanced up, before giving full attention to the game. Since he wasn't invited to join, Revill went to his pallet and lay down with his hands beneath his head.

After a while he appeared to doze off; only Shearer would have suspected otherwise.

***

Following a few days' sojourn at West Dean, the Queen's Progress at last reached Chichester, and few were more relieved than Revill. Though had he an inkling as to what would follow in the days to come, he would think later, he might have been better prepared.

As it was, he rode Malachi around the walls and thence through the east gate into this small city, and could not help but admire its beauty. Lying on a Roman road beside the river Lavant, the old town basked in warm evening sunlight, with the tower of St Richard's Minster ahead. Paved streets lined with thatched houses stretched away in several directions, as Lord Ballater's party came to a slow halt. The sea was but half a dozen miles away, Revill had heard; he believed he could smell it.

The Queen and her retinue had already bypassed Chichester by some miles, making for the house of Lord Lumley who would be her host for the duration. Other noblemen would stay nearby, within the town and its surrounds. And for once, even Ballater had acquired good accommodation. Or rather, Harman had ridden ahead and arranged it, claiming it was needed for an important member of the Queen's train. The house, in the south-east quarter, though not large was elegant enough, built on the grounds of a former monastery. Even His Lordship seemed satisfied, as he stood outside the doorway and looked up at the latticed windows.

The other men had dismounted while Hawkins backed the cart up towards the house. Then a figure appeared from inside, bowed and murmured a welcome. Revill saw an elderly man, soberly dressed, with strands of white hair struggling to cover his baldness.

'This is Master Bridges, my Lord,' Harman said. 'He exports malt. He'll be honoured to host you.' Turning to Bridges, he announced that his guest was Lord Ballater. The man nodded politely.

'Malt, eh?' His Lordship eyed his new host. 'I'm intrigued... but for now, I'd like to repair to my chamber and take some rest. Do you have any passable sack in the house?'

'I do, sir.' The old man glanced past him, and his face fell somewhat. 'Do I take it I should accommodate your followers too?'

'Don't concern ourself about them - they'll sleep anywhere,' was the gruff reply. 'Though my steward would like a chamber. Do you have another to spare?'

'I believe I can find one,' Bridges replied. 'I'll instruct my servants - will you enter?'

Ballater nodded, then looked round for Harman. The steward had gone to his horse, and now returned with a stout cane which he handed to his master. Revill hadn't noticed it before today, but when His Lordship took it and leaned upon it, he knew: Ballater was feeling frail, and had ordered a stick for walking. As he ascended the steps and entered the house, he gave a wheezing cough before disappearing from sight.

'There's a stable and an outhouse at the back,' Harman said, eyeing Revill and Shearer. 'Best settle in. I'll be dining with His Lordship. You can fadge for yourselves, eh?'

With that, the burly steward followed his master indoors. Revill glanced at Shearer, then at Hawkins, who had climbed down from the cart. And for once, at sight of Harman's smug expression, the three of them shared a brief moment of camaraderie.

'Help me unload, and we'll find an inn,' Hawkins said, looking dusty and weary after their journey. 'I'll even buy you both a mug.'

The other two exchanged looks, and almost smiled.

***

The tavern was the King's Head in South Street, as crowded as any other establishment had been along the path of Queen Elizabeth's Progress. The three of them – all soldiers or ex-soldiers, Revill realised – managed to squeeze into a corner table where they bespoke a good supper. Having satisfied their appetites, they fell upon the house ale. Revill and Shearer, wary of over-indulging, drank sparingly – but Master Hawkins, it seemed, was in a different humour. In fact, for some reason the man was almost talkative.

'He's starting to rattle me,' he muttered, after taking a generous pull from his tankard. And when the other two looked nonplussed: 'Harman, I mean - who did you think?'

'I thought you meant His Lordship,' Shearer said. 'He can be difficult, can he not?'

'Oh, I'm used to his ways,' Hawkins growled. 'But Master Steward, now...' He frowned. 'Things were never the same after he was raised to the post, back home. And since this Progress began, he's puffed himself up all the more.'

'He has a lot on his mind, I suppose,' Revill put in casually. He had been watching the man, and seen a look he recognised:

A RELUCTANT HERO

Hawkins, he decided, was of a mind to get drunk. Whether that might prove useful, or merely troublesome, he was unsure.

'But that's how he likes it,' Hawkins said. 'Now he's got his own chamber. Next thing we know he'll be riding with His Lordship over to Stansted, drinking sack instead of ale.'

'Stansted – isn't that Lord Lumley's seat?' Shearer enquired.

'It is. Stansted Park, a big house built over an old hunting lodge. The Queen's father once hunted there, they say, and so will she.'

Revill listened closely. He had heard of Lord John Lumley, a man of ancient lineage – and now he remembered: like Lord Ballater, the man was a Catholic.

'Is our master acquainted with Lumley?' He asked. On a sudden, his mind was active.

'I believe so,' Hawkins replied, before taking another drink. With a frown, and added: 'I know what you're thinking – noblemen of our religion stick together like glue. Downtrodden and bitter men, eh? Well, Lumley isn't that sort.'

At that, Revill and Shearer exchanged looks which Hawkins failed to notice. On impulse, Revill took up the jug of ale and refilled the man's mug.

'Then what sort is he?' He prompted. 'For if I recall correctly, he was once caught up in a conspiracy over the Queen of Scots. Even went to prison – or so I heard.'

'That was twenty years back,' Hawkins countered. 'And later on, he was one of the judges at her trial. Hardly the act of a traitor, is it? He learned his lesson. He keeps himself out of trouble - as we all must.'

'Wise man,' Shearer said.

A moment passed. Revill had called for a pipe of tobacco, which a harassed drawer now brought over, making apology for the delay. Revill paid him and busied himself lighting up. Meanwhile Hawkins, becoming somewhat flushed in the hot room, continued to drink.

'Made himself poorer, though,' he murmured, almost to himself. 'Like the rest of them.'

'The rest of them?' Revill paused, puffing at the pipe.

'Aye - men like my master,' came the reply. 'He's poor as a beggar. Don't you think he'd be travelling with a bigger train than us, if he could afford to?'

'It crossed my mind,' Shearer put in. 'But it's not my habit to judge. I was asked to serve a peer of the realm, and so I do - like Perrot here.'

'And you've no scruples about letting a Papist buy you a drink,' Hawkins sneered.

'Better than that,' Revill said. 'I'm buying another jug. I take it you've no scruples about sharing it with a Protestant?'

At that Hawkins gave a snort – then, to the surprise of both his fellows, let out a sudden laugh. It was the first time either of them had seen him crack a smile.

'I'll drink further with you, Perrot,' he said, with a nod. 'As any old soldier would. I'll even compare scars, if you like.'

'No need for that.' Revill blew out a stream of blue smoke. 'I trust you.'

Hawkins peered at him through the smoke. 'Are you jesting with me?'

'Not at all.' He looked round for the drawer and signalled for more ale. Then he caught Shearer's gaze: he too, it seemed, might wish to use this opportunity to gain intelligence, but was urging caution. Revill threw him a slight nod and turned back to Hawkins.

'So the Queen will hunt, as Lord Lumley's guest,' he said, putting on a wry smile. 'Though I can't see our master joining the party, given his... shape. Or the speed of his horse.'

'It wouldn't stop him trying, if he were invited,' Hawkins said. 'He was a hunting man when he was younger. And Lumley's no youth himself.' He gave a sigh, picked up his mug and drained it. With a careless air, Revill poured the remaining contents of the jug into it. A moment passed, then:

'This country's become a stool-pit.' Hawkins was glowering down at the table. 'No honour anywhere... a Queen who cares only for jewels and fancy frocks and dancing, and a populace too addle-pated to do aught but fawn over her. It's enough to make a man weep.'

A RELUCTANT HERO

'Why do you stay, then?' Shearer enquired. 'You could live elsewhere, among men of your own faith.'

'By the Lord, I could!' On a sudden, the man brought his fist down on the table. One or two people glanced round, then ignored him: just a man growing maudlin with drink.

'Ireland,' Hawkins said. 'I fought over there, you know.' He eyed Revill. 'With Lord Grey ten years back, in the Desmond rebellion. Fought against men of my own faith... and I've regretted it ever since.' Fiercely, he looked up. 'Don't you have regrets, Perrot? About those you killed – soldiers who fought for what they thought was right, like you did?'

'I do,' Revill said, after a moment.

'I'd a mind to desert,' the other went on, barely listening. 'Join the Irish kerns, and live in the true faith. If I'd got caught, what could they do but hang me? But by the grace of God, at least I'd go off with a clean conscience.'

He paused and reached for his mug, then after drinking sat nursing it between his palms. In spite of everything, Revill pitied him. And once again, the thought came to his mind: this man was no villain, bent on threatening the Queen's life. Despite the difference in religion, the yawning gulf that lay between them, he knew Hawkins; he had seen others like him. Underneath the hard-baked exterior, he was a fair man.

Which left Harman as the only suspect... and he too seemed a most unlikely assassin. In that instant, doubt arose: was Sir Robert Cecil merely so suspicious that it clouded his judgement? Was he seeing conspiracies where, on this occasion at least, none existed?

'But you didn't,' Shearer said then, breaking Revill's thoughts. 'Desert, I mean.' He was eying Hawkins, frankly and without rancour.

'No - in the end, I couldn't,' came the reply. 'I liked Lord Grey... and I saw comrades die, men I'd come to respect. So I did my part, and came home like the rest; those who could, that is. Besides, there was a woman waiting for me... or so I thought.'

All three of them were silent after that, until a drawer appeared with the jug and plonked it down hurriedly. In doing so, some of the ale spilled out on to the table. At once, Hawkins gave a start and lurched to his feet.

'Dolt!' He cried, glaring at the man. 'There's a good mouthful there!'

'Your pardon,' the drawer muttered. 'I'm a mite rushed tonight-'

'Rushed, are you?' Hawkins lifted a hand and pointed. 'Well then, you can rush off and fetch another mugful, free of charge!'

The man blanched, looking round for assistance. To his relief Revill and Shearer rose as one, ready to avert trouble. Their companion had turned on a coin from maudlin to aggressive: a phenomenon familiar enough to them both.

'That'll be all,' Revill said to the drawer. Without delay, the man hurried off.

'What are you doing?' Somewhat blearily, Hawkins turned on him. 'They should make good the wastage, so they should. Are you scared of a tussle, or-'

'Don't you think you've drunk enough for now?' Shearer broke in, placing a restraining hand on his arm. 'No cause for a brabble, is there?'

'Who asked you?' Came the retort. 'I'll fight any of these folk – you too, if need be!'

'Matthew, isn't that your name?' Revill said calmly. 'Come then, Matthew, and think what'll happen if His Lordship hears. Or do you want to end up in the town lock-up?'

Hawkins scowled at him. 'They'd have to take me first,' he retorted. 'And what's that about His Lordship? You'd tell him, would you? You blasted rogue, I'll-'

But that was all he said. Abruptly the inn had gone quiet, all eyes turned in the direction of the fracas. From the corner of his eye, Revill saw two of the drawers urging another man to his feet: a constable, by the look of him. As the three of them started forwards, customers fell back. There was some muttering, along with a few hostile looks: the trio of armed men were strangers here - and heavily outnumbered.

'Peace – we'll take him out,' Revill said loudly. Whereupon he and Shearer grasped Hawkins by the shoulders, drew him from the

A RELUCTANT HERO

table and began to steer him through the throng. One or two men were on their feet, but mercifully no-one stood in the way. Soon they had reached the door, under the eyes of the constable who stood near.

'Your pardon, master,' Shearer said with a forced grin. 'Our friend is out of sorts. With your leave we'll see him safely to his bed. Will that serve?'

Whereupon, without waiting for answer he and Revill shoved Hawkins out of the door, ignoring his angry and slurred mutterings. Once in the street, they picked up pace and hurried him away. But as they moved off Revill glanced round… and stiffened.

Three men, a cut above the average by their clothes, emerged from a side-street in a group, heading for the door of the King's Head. In conversation, they paid little attention to the sight of passers-by, arm-in-arm and seemingly merry with drink.

But Revill had recognised two of them: the Crown Purveyors, Godwin and Hooper.

EIGHT

The following morning, when most of Lord Ballater's company had slept late, there came an announcement. His Lordship, it seemed, had a desire to look at the quay which served as a landing stage for merchandise in and out of Chichester. The place was called Appledram, on account of the good soil thereabouts for apple growing. Revill, standing near the outhouse which had been hastily cleared out and was now his quarters, took in the news without interest - until Harman told him that he was expected to come along.

'My Lord has given his instructions,' he said. 'If he wants to get down, he'll need help.' But for Revill, his expression seemed to tell a different tale: the steward was being as good as his word, and didn't want to let him out of his sight.

'Who else is coming?' He asked. But when answer came, he was surprised: their host Master Bridges would accompany them. The quay, it turned out, was a place from where he shipped his malt. More surprising still was the news that Lord Ballater had shown an interest in the man's business.

'You, Shearer and I will be the escort,' Harman added. 'Hawkins is... not quite himself.'

To that, Revill needed no explanation: he knew the ex-soldier had taken too much drink, with obvious consequences. He went off to saddle Malachi.

A short while later the party left Chichester by its south gate, crossed a bridge and rode two miles through pleasant country, downriver to Appledram. Revill and Shearer, who had ridden together in silence, found themselves almost at the mouth of the Lavant, where the estuary widened considerably. There was a wharf with a hut, and a few sacks of grain piled up. A boat was moored at the quay, its cargo covered with sailcloth, but no-one was in sight. Ballater reined in, puffing in the saddle, and looked about.Hugh Bridges, the malt merchant, drew to a halt beside him.

A RELUCTANT HERO

By now, Master Bridges had aroused Revill's curiosity. He was a childless widower, it had transpired, somewhat deaf and slow, who looked uncomfortable playing host to a nobleman like Ballater. His Lordship meanwhile, despite his somewhat lowly standing among peers of the realm, was behaving with increasing bombast. Bridges' modest household boasted few servants, yet they still out-numbered Ballater's. Even so, when taking breakfast in the kitchens that morning, it had become clear to Revill that Ballater had managed to dominate the house, demanding a breakfast in his chamber. Harman, seeing how the land lay, was also asserting himself. Sitting his horse this morning, he wore what looked like a smile of satisfaction.

'I'll get down,' His Lordship said, looking round. 'Hurry up, you men.'

Revill and Shearer dismounted, let their reins trail and went to help him. Harman, however, remained horsed. Without a third pair of hands, it took considerable effort to get their master out of the saddle. Turning about, His Lordship then called for his stick, which Harman was holding out. Shearer went to take it and brought it over.

'Well now, Master Bridges.' Taking the cane and leaning on it, Ballater looked to his host, who was also dismounting. Bridges, though a man of similar age, was given no assistance. His Lordship, clearly in expansive mood, urged him to assume the role of guide.

'This is known as Dell Quay,' Bridges said in his reedy voice. 'My produce leaves here for many places: westward to Portsmouth and beyond, and eastward as far as London. We're famous hereabouts for our malthouses.'

'Indeed?' Ballater was smiling. 'Most profitable, I'm sure.'

'I'll allow, I have no cause to complain,' came the unassuming reply.

Revill glanced at Bridges, as mild a man of business as he had ever seen. The London merchants he had known were as hard-headed and grasping as any in Europe, but this elderly townsman seemed almost apologetic for his status which, to judge by his house, his servants and the horses Revill had seen in the stable, suggested a man of some success. He was musing on it as Harman, having now dismounted, brushed past him.

'Portsmouth, did I hear you say?' The steward addressed Bridges. 'How long does the journey take from here, eh?'

'It's but four leagues distant... more if the wind is against you. And it depends on the tide,' the man replied, with some hesitancy. 'It's quicker to ride... were you not intending to follow the Queen, wherever she goes?'

'Of course we are,' Ballater said quickly, throwing his steward a disapproving look for butting in. His gaze shifted to Revill and Shearer, who stood aside without expression.

'Master Bridges and I will talk now,' he announced to no-one in particular. 'I didn't come here merely to take the air. Give way, the rest of you.'

And with that His Lordship took a few paces along the wharf. Bridges accompanied him, the two of them soon out of earshot. Looking somewhat disgruntled, Harman moved to join the other two.

'Surely My Lord isn't thinking of going into the malting business?' Shearer said. And when Harman turned swiftly to him: 'Some nobles do, don't they? Though from what I know, it involves considerable investment.'

'What?' A glare appeared on the steward's face. 'Are you implying something?'

'I?' Shearer's face was blank. 'Heaven forfend... merely idle speculation.'

'Indeed? Well, along with your soldiers' gossip, idle speculation can get a man into trouble,' Harman retorted. 'And, was that a smirk?'

He was addressing Revill, who raised his eyebrows. 'I never smirk,' he said.

The steward met his eye, then turned to Shearer... whereupon he stiffened and dropped his gaze. But they understood well enough: this man's authority existed solely at the whim of his master. Harman was not such a brave man, and either of these two - under his orders by mere force of circumstance - could have bettered him with ease.

A RELUCTANT HERO

After that, nothing more was said. The steward moved aside, gazing downriver. Revill went over to Malachi and took a costrel from his saddle-pack. It contained watered ale, somewhat tepid but welcome enough on a summer morning.

'What's this, I wonder?' Having taken a drink, Shearer returned the vessel to Revill and jerked his head towards Ballater and Bridges, who were regarding the boat. 'His Lordship's poor as a palliard – and he's no merchant. Fit for shouting orders and little else. I don't believe he cares a fig for Bridges, or his malt.'

'I don't either,' Revill said. 'More, I'm certain Harman knows it.'

'Have you come to any conclusions about him?'

'I just can't see him as an assassin. Clumsy, and not the brightest candle in the church.'

Shearer nodded. Last night, while Hawkins slept soundly in a corner of the outhouse, the two of them had talked at length about Revill's mission, about Cecil, and Heneage too. Neither of them, however, had a clear idea how to proceed. Shearer, as loyal to the Crown as anyone, now shared Revill's doubts about an attempt on the Queen's life. Though there were some in England who would relish the chance, no-one in Ballater's party seemed capable. And there was the curious matter of Dickon, now revealed to be His Lordship's son.

'I can't fathom it,' Shearer admitted. 'Though when it comes to English Catholics, I never could. At one end you've got fanatics like Babbington, men who'll go to the gallows swearing allegiance to the Pope. At the other, seemingly law-abiding men like Anthony Browne who seem determined to prove their loyalty to the Queen. But in the middle…'

'In the middle are those who blow with the wind,' Revill finished. 'Keep out of trouble, like the Queen's new host Lord Lumley. But if a great blow was struck, such as a Spanish invasion, who knows?'

'I know some would rejoice,' Shearer said. 'Perhaps even a majority.'

They fell silent, sharing the ale. Some distance away, Ballater and his new friend Bridges appeared to be deep in conversation.

Harman meanwhile was growing restless, glancing at his master from time to time. Revill was taking another drink when there came a noise of hooves from behind, prompting him to turn sharply.

Two riders were approaching, descending the shallow slope to the quayside. One of the men was a stranger to Revill; the other was Nicholas Godwin.

There was no greeting. Godwin drew rein a short distance away, then sat his horse looking first at Revill, then at Shearer. His companion did likewise, with frank curiosity. After a moment, Revill bent close to his fellow and murmured an explanation. Whereupon Master Harman took it upon himself to intervene, coming forward and bidding the newcomers good morning. The sentiment was returned in perfunctory fashion, then:

'Still bumbling about, Perrot?' Godwin's words were heavy with sarcasm. 'I had a mind you'd be at Stansted now, hobnobbing with grander folk.'

'As you know, I serve His Lordship,' Revill said mildly, with a nod towards Ballater. 'Though I'm curious as to what brings you down here. Business, is it?'

'Of course,' came the swift reply. 'I too am at my work.' He indicated the boat.

'Is anything valuable aboard?' Revill enquired. 'If so, it seems odd that it's unguarded.'

'Depends on whether you call barrels of fish and oysters valuable,' Godwin returned. 'I'm here to see them unloaded... there's a cart following.'

Harman, who had grown displeased at the exchange, put his oar in. 'Do you men know each other?' He demanded of Revill.

'Of course - we're old friends!' Godwin said immediately. 'Shared a chamber once. Rivals for the same woman too, though I was the winner of that particular bout – eh, Perrot?'

The air was tense now, Harman shifting his gaze from one to the other. Shearer, standing solidly beside Revill, wore a look of warning, following which Godwin's companion leaned across to him from the saddle and spoke briefly. Now, Revill recognised him as the other man he had seen the previous night, walking in

A RELUCTANT HERO

Chichester with Godwin and Hooper. And the more he saw, the less he liked: another one of Hooper's ilk, he decided.

But the tension was broken suddenly by Lord Ballater. At his shout all the men turned to see him puffing towards them, waving his stick. Bridges followed behind.

'What's this, a flock of gossiping hens?' His Lordship cried. 'We're done here, and will ride back. Master Steward?'

It was a relief, and at once Harman moved to attend him. Revill and Shearer turned away from Godwin and his fellow and were soon occupied in getting their master into the saddle. Meanwhile, the Crown Purchasers dismounted and moved past them to stand beside the boat. As Revill took up Malachi's rein and prepared to mount, there was a rumble of wheels: looking round, he saw that Godwin had spoken truly: a cart was approaching, drawn by a single ox. The cargo of fish would be unloaded and carried away.

And yet, Revill would no more have trusted Godwin now – or his companion - than he would have trusted a cornered rat. As he got himself mounted, he threw a glance in that one's direction and received a look in return: one of hostility. In his bones, he knew that this was not the last time he would see these men – and likely their angry friend Hooper, too.

Turning away, he and Shearer allowed Lord Ballater and Bridges to ride away from Dell's Quay, passing the cart where the driver doffed his cap. Then they were following, without looking back.

***

That same night, matters came to a head.

After supper Revill sat in the kitchen with Shearer and Hawkins, who had now returned to being his taciturn self. Ballater and Harman, meanwhile, were dining in the best chamber with their host, prompting a good deal of toing and froing from servants carrying various dishes. Wine too was being called for, it seemed, in some abundance.

'I hope Master Bridges keeps a well-stocked cellar,' Shearer remarked. 'At this rate, His Lordship will drink it dry.'

Revill merely shrugged, while Hawkins' mind, it seemed, was elsewhere. Following his gaze, Revill saw a rather plump, smiling kitchen maid looking in their direction. And one look at Hawkins' face was enough: the man was sorely tempted.

'Someone caught your eye?' He murmured.

'Eh?' Hawkins turned to frown at him. 'What's it to you?'

'Why, it's nothing to me,' Revill replied.

'Nor me,' Shearer put in, with his practised air of innocence. 'A man must take his pleasures where he finds them – especially an old soldier, eh? By the look of her, you've made an impression.'

A moment passed, before Hawkins decided to ignore his fellows and return his attention to the woman. She was about to resume her duties, but before turning away, she threw a look at him that could not be mistaken. In reply he managed a grin… and soon after that, rose from the table.

'Have a care – and don't wake me up when you come to your own bed,' Shearer said.

There was no answer from Hawkins, who made his way to the open door and disappeared. His companions faced each other and exchanged smiles.

Around an hour later, after going to the stables to look in on Malachi, Revill walked across the yard back to the outhouse. Having been used for storage the place stank of malt, which he was trying to get accustomed to. The single, shuttered window was wide open, and as they had done the previous night the men kept the door ajar, wedged with a stone. On entering the dim-lit interior he found Shearer settling down for the night, and Hawkins still absent.

'I hope Harman doesn't get to know of it,' Shearer said. 'He seems to think we should forgo any pleasures for the sake of service to his esteemed Lordship. While just now, I suspect a different kind of service is going on not far from here, somewhere private.'

Revill sat down on his pallet and pulled off his shoes. 'Have you a notion what duties our master has for us tomorrow?' He asked, letting out a yawn. 'More sight-seeing?'

'God knows,' came the tired reply. With that, Shearer turned to snuff out the single candle and rolled into his blanket. Outside, darkness was falling. Somewhere a bell tolled, and the city was still; Chichester folk, it seemed, went to bed early. Soon Revill was dozing, thrusting aside darker thoughts for ones of Jenna, who after a day's toil at the farm would be asleep already. As his eyes closed, he pictured her in bed... and envied Hawkins, wherever he was.

He had been asleep for what seemed only minutes when he awoke - and smelled smoke.

At once he sat up, peering about in the gloom. Nearby Shearer shifted in his sleep; there was no sound from the direction of Hawkins' pallet. Rising quickly, Revill stumbled towards the door – and found it was closed; moreover, when he pushed it, it wouldn't yield. Then he saw flames, creeping under the bottom of the timbers... and smoke rose, curling about him.

'Shearer! Hawkins!' He shouted, stepping back. 'Fire!'

'Do you jest?' Shearer exclaimed, from out of the dark. A muttered oath followed as he rose. Coming forward in his stockinged feet, he shoved at the door, but it failed to move.

'It's been barred from without,' Revill said, standing close to him. 'It's deliberate.'

With another oath, Shearer blundered in the direction of the window – and only now did both of them realise the shutters were closed. When they tried to open it, Revill's words proved true: the window too was barred.

'Hawkins!' Shearer yelled. 'Wake up, we need to get out!'

There was no answer... and on a sudden, a suspicion flew to Revill's mind. Groping forward in the gloom, he reached Hawkins' pallet – and found that it was empty.

'He's not here.'

'To hades with him, then,' Shearer replied. 'We'll have to force our way...' But with a cough, he broke off. The smoke was increasing, and if this continued they could be overcome... which, Revill now knew, was precisely what someone intended.

'I'll start on the window,' he called out. 'Will you try and douse the flames?'

His answer was a grunt and more stumbling about. But moving rapidly, the two of them set to work. While Shearer brought his blanket and threw it down at the base of the door, stamping and coughing in the smoke, Revill found his poniard and hurried back to the window. Thrusting it between the shutters, he was able to gain leverage – until, as he put his weight behind it, the blade broke. With a curse he fell back, just as a tongue of red flame showed at the gap. Now he saw it: the entire front of the outhouse was on fire.

'It's no use!' He shouted. 'The door is our only chance.'

'Let's to it, then!' Shearer's cry was hoarse. He began battering at the door, but it remained immoveable, nor had his efforts at staunching the flames had any success; if anything, the fire burned fiercer. Both of them felt the heat of it now, as smoke swirled, stinging their eyes. From outside, Revill thought he heard shouts... surely someone would come to their aid?

'We must throw ourselves at it together,' he said, coming close to Shearer. 'On the count of three?' And when the other grunted agreement he began: 'One, two – now!'

Using all their body-weight, both men fell against the door - which gave a little, but still held. Again Revill counted, and again they crashed against the stout timbers, bruising arms and shoulders. This time there was movement, and a crack of wood... coughing, they drew back for a final attempt - whereupon Shearer turned about in confusion.

'What in God's name are you doing?' He shouted. 'Come back here!'

But Revill, saving his breath, made no answer. He was on his knees beside his pallet, fumbling for his shoes. Time was running out, and he saw only one solution. Having managed to put the shoes on – on the wrong feet, he would discover later – he got up and stumbled back to the door.

'Move,' he muttered. And before his companion could utter a protest, he had shoved him aside. Judging the distance as best he could, he then turned round, raised his leg and aimed a violent back-kick at the door, connecting with a loud thud. He followed it with several more kicks, using alternate heels - and at last, the door began to give. But he was growing weaker, blinded by smoke, sweat pouring down his face. Holding his breath, he gathered his strength for more kicks – until he was thrown aside, falling to the floor.

The assault was followed by a wild cry as Shearer flew past him, smashing into the door with abandon, to be rewarded by a great splintering of timbers. Following which, Revill was seized by the arm and dragged through wreckage and flames – to find himself out in the yard, gulping night air, while about him mayhem raged: shouts and cries, figures darting about… then he was on his back, aware that someone was lying beside him. His eyes streaming, he turned to see Shearer, gasping and retching… but alive.

Once again, it seemed, Cecil's man had probably saved his life.

NINE

Morning brought peace, of a sort; it also brought recriminations.

It was a city watchman, it transpired, who had first raised the alarm: a faint glow of flame visible from the rear of Hugh Bridges' house. By the time he had alerted the household, however, the fire had gained a strong hold. Servants had emerged in their nightclothes, among them the cook who had the presence to lower buckets down the stable-yard well. Harman had also come out of the house, shouting and blustering but adding little to the rescue effort. Three men were known to be sleeping in the old malt store, but why they hadn't woken and got out was a mystery until later, when a discovery was made: the door of the building had been wedged shut with beams of oak. The window shutters too had been wedged tight... which left little doubt as to what had occurred.

At first, no-one wanted to admit it; but Revill and Shearer, scratched, bruised and seared after their ordeal, their clothes ruined, knew better than anyone that it was no accident.

'But in God's name, why?'

It was Lord Ballater who spoke, when he and his people assembled in the front room of the house, along with a shocked Master Bridges. Order had been restored, hurts tended and the victims of the blaze clothed. The outhouse was still standing, even if one side was burnt out; it was sheer luck that only part of the thatch was lost. Fears that the fire might have spread to the stable had been allayed by the quick-thinking cook and his team of bucket-wielders. Mercifully, once the flames had been doused, Reville and Shearer had managed to retrieve their swords and valuables from the blackened interior. But there was no possibility of their being billeted in the outhouse again.

'I cannot fathom it, My Lord.'

Harman, seated at a table beside his master, shook his head. Reville, standing with Shearer, kept his eyes averted; he harboured suspicions, but had no intention of sharing them yet.

A RELUCTANT HERO

'You - what do you say, master bodyguard?'

Realising that His Lordship was addressing him – and more, that there was hostility in his voice – Revill looked up.

'A fanatic… someone who hates Catholics, my Lord,' he suggested. 'And likely assumes that all your servants share the same faith.'

'Whereas,' Shearer put in coolly, 'one who does share it missed all the excitement. Fortune smiled on him, perhaps-'

'What insolence!'

It was Harman, interrupting him angrily. 'What do you mean?' He demanded. 'Wherever Hawkins was, I know him as an honest man! If I thought otherwise, I'd-'

But it was the steward's turn to be cut short, as Ballater broke in. Red-faced and short-tempered, he now appeared more alarmed by the near-disaster than Revill had realised.

'Enough!' He snapped. 'This may be a farrago, but it could have been worse. Though heaven knows what'll happen if Her Majesty and her Councillors hear of it…' Abruptly he turned to Bridges, and waited until the man faced him.

'And yet the truth is, this reflects most badly on you, sir. Does it not?'

At that, an awkward silence fell. Harman looked down, his eyes on the table. But Lord Ballater, his gaze fixed squarely on his host, merely awaited a reply. For his part, Bridges merely stared before giving way to an expression of dismay.

'By heaven, sir,' he murmured, 'how can you say such a thing?'

'I say it because it's true,' His Lordship retorted. 'I'm your guest - a nobleman in the Queen's train – and I have been put in grave danger. Along with my servants, of course,' he added. 'You should have had a guard posted. What if the house had been set on fire, and I with no means of escape, eh?'

'But that's absurd,' his host protested. 'The blaze was clearly set at the malthouse, and nowhere else. Though how the… the fire-starters gained entry troubles me sorely. Climbed over the wall, perhaps-'

'What does it matter how the varlets got in?' Ballater interrupted. 'If I didn't know better, I might even suspect they had some assistance from within - a bribe to a servant, from some business rival of yours, perhaps? I've known such things happen.'

'But I haven't an enemy in the world – I swear it!' Aghast now, Bridges put a hand to his forehead. 'This is cruel, sir. I protest, in the strongest terms…'

He trailed off, whereupon a new voice spoke up.

'My Lord, if you please.'

All eyes turned to Shearer, who clearly felt he had been silent long enough.

'Well?' Ballater eyed him. 'What have you to say now?'

'With respect, sir, I say that trying to apportion blame is fruitless,' Shearer answered in a level tone. 'Perrot and I escaped, and no-one has been harmed. Likely the Queen's train will move on soon, and any danger to Master Bridges and his household will pass. Assuming it was your company who brought it upon him, that is-'

'You rogue – how dare you!'

Cutting him short, His Lordship rose unsteadily to his feet, letting out a cough as he did so. At once, the other men braced themselves for an onslaught on Shearer for his boldness… until the door opened and a figure appeared, stunning everyone to silence.

In walked Hawkins, looking unkempt and very sheepish.

Nobody spoke. After a quick glance round at the assembled company, Hawkins made a bow from which he seemed in no hurry to rise. When he finally did so, he faced his master and murmured something inaudible.

'What's that?' In mingled surprise and relief, Ballater stared at him.

'I begged your pardon, My Lord,' Hawkins said. 'I was… the matter is, I got called away last night and, well…'

'What do you mean?' His Lordship frowned. 'I demand answer!'

Now the tension was palpable. Hawkins hesitated, while Harman, who seemed to feel he might be blamed in some way, looked angry. Meanwhile Master Bridges gazed from one man to another, blinking in alarm - until on impulse, Revill decided to

A RELUCTANT HERO

intervene. He was unsure where the notion sprang from, but he thought it might be expedient.

'Your pardon, my Lord, but if I may?' And when every man turned to him: 'I believe I can offer an explanation for Master Hawkins' absence from the outhouse. For in truth, he was only acting at my request.'

His answer was another silence. Beside him, Shearer let out a sigh that was closer to a moan. Hawkins' eyes swung towards Revill.

'Your request?' Ballater's frown deepened.

'I was supposed to meet someone,' Revill said, thinking fast. 'But when I went to the stable to see to my horse, I was distracted. I feared he might be unwell, though it turned out to be naught... yet in any case, the hour was late. It's my place to guard you, so... well, Hawkins agreed to take a message for me. Afterwards he, er...'

But he trailed off, all too aware of the lameness of the tale. Silently, he berated himself for his foolishness. A moment passed... and then the dam broke.

'You devil! You blasted varlet!'

Revill froze, his gaze on His Lordship.

'What a pottage of lies!' Lord Ballater fumed. 'Do you think me such a fool as to believe such? Meet someone, you say – so you would have left me unguarded? And now you seek to draw Hawkins into your treachery? By the saints, I'd...'

But there, the tirade ended.

With a cough Ballater flinched, drew a rattling breath, then sank down on to his chair. Sweat was on his brow as he fumbled for a kerchief – to be produced by Harman, who leaped to attend him. Still coughing, His Lordship put a hand to his mouth while Hawkins seized a cup from the table and brought it to him. Ballater took it shakily, drank, then set it down with a thud. Finally, when the others showed relief that the fit had passed, he raised a hand and pointed at Revill.

'Get out, Perrot,' he ordered, breathing hard. 'You're dismissed from my service. In truth I never wanted you in the first place - whatever Sir Hunchback Cecil might have said. Collect your belongings and leave, and I pray I never set eyes upon you again. Go!'

And so, it was done; Revill's two weeks' attendance on Lord Ballater was at an end. What might follow, he had no notion; a jumble of thoughts flew up, some involving possible plots against the Queen, but it was too late. Without a word, and without making a bow, he took a last look round at the company. All, apart from His Lordship, appeared dumbfounded.

Then he was walking out through the door, which Hawkins had left open.

***

Feeling the need of a drink and a pipe, he went to the King's Head in South Street. There was a small stable behind the inn, with a stall for Malachi; many townsfolk, he learned, had left Chichester for a glimpse of the Queen who was hunting at Stansted. Relieved to be alone, with no need to pretend any more, Revill sat at the same table he, Shearer and Hawkins had shared two days ago and drank. Then he leaned back against the wall, and tried to think.

His first thought was that he should try and see Cecil; then he remembered that the man had ordered him not to make contact. Some means must be found to get a message to him, however – and his only go-between was Shearer. How his companion would deal with his abrupt departure, he had no idea; likely he would think that he had to remain at Bridges' house to continue watching Ballater's train. Though for Revill, the notion remained that neither Hawkins nor Harman were plausible assassins. Once again, he was forced to the conclusion that Cecil's suspicions were unfounded. What, then, was to be done?

He was still sitting in the King's Head an hour later, having turned matters about to no avail, when Hawkins came in.

'I had a notion you might be here,' he said as he approached the table. Taken aback, Revill merely gazed at him.

'I don't have long,' the ex-soldier added. 'I'm on an errand... are you hungry?'

'Not very,' Revill answered, after a moment. 'But you can buy me a mug if you like.'

A RELUCTANT HERO

Hawkins nodded and signalled to the drawer. Fortunately, it was a different man from the one he had threatened the last time he was here. Catching up a stool from nearby, he sat himself down.

'I'd a mind to thank you,' he began. 'For what you tried to do, back at the house.'

Revill shrugged, then put on a wry look. 'I hope the wench was worth it.'

'Well now, there's the puzzlement,' came the reply. 'As it happens, she never appeared.'

'Oh?' Revill frowned. 'So, where were you all those hours?'

'That's a good question,' Hawkins said. He looked round as the drawer came up, and ordered mugs of beer for them both.

'It was a ruse,' he went on, when the man had gone. 'She - the maid that is, name of Margaret – met me outside the kitchen and told me to go to the alehouse by the Greyfriars, where she was known and could get a room.' He gave a sigh. 'Like a dolt, I believed her.'

'And what happened then?' Revill wanted to know.

'What happened was, soon as I walked into that grimy little rathole, this cove accosts me and asks if I'm here to meet with Margaret. When I said I was, he said she'd be along soon, and would I take a drink? And more fool me, I did, whereupon…'

'It was laced,' Revill finished; on a sudden, his mind was busy.

'By the Christ, it must have been,' Hawkins said. 'For next thing I know, the sun's up and I'm sprawled on the floor, mouth like old leather and my head beating marching-time. More, the bastard who gave me the drink's nowhere to be seen, the landlord says he knows nothing, and throws me out as if I was just any oaf who'd overdrunk! How's that for a night's pleasure?' He gave a sigh. 'So, I got myself back to the house, and you know what followed.'

'Not all of it, I don't,' Revill said. 'What of the maid – did you not go looking for her?'

'I did – and here's where it gets more puzzling. Seems she just helps out now and then, when Bridges has guests. No-one's seen her since yesterday.'

On a sudden he looked up. 'I was led astray, was I not? Someone wanted me out of the way for the night, leaving you and Shearer to-'

'Leaving us to die,' Revill finished.

Hawkins blinked, but had no answer.

'What of Shearer?' Revill asked then. 'Is he staying, or what?'

'Looks like it. Him and me have been given a chamber under the eaves, to share for the duration. I don't know how long that'll be. There's been no word from Stansted, but I'll tell you this: I can't get out of Chichester quick enough.'

'And His Lordship?'

Hawkins shrugged. 'He's in no hurry. Still has a notion about presenting his petition to the Queen, but I can't see that being allowed. And besides, he's-'

'A sick man,' Revill broke in, and received a nod in reply.

'But see now...' On a sudden, Hawkins was frowning. 'Who wanted you dead, Perrot? Who'd go to all that trouble, breaking in and doing what they did? I'm a mite curious – and Shearer won't talk about it, which makes me more curious.'

'Let's say I've made a few enemies in my time,' Revill replied, after a moment.

'You must have. And not the cleverest of enemies, I'd say... did they think no-one would see the door and window had been barricaded? It's a matter of arson, not to say attempted murder - gallows stuff.'

Revill gave no answer. When the drawer appeared, he took his mug and drank at once.

'Well then, what will you do now?' Hawkins asked, picking up his own drink.

'You said you'd a mind to thank me,' Revill said, after a pause. 'Will you do a small service instead? Will you take a message back to Shearer?' And when the other hesitated: 'It's important to me.'

'If it is, then I'll do it.'

Relaxing somewhat, Revill nodded his thanks. He got up, moved across the room to the drawer and requested ink, a quill and a scrap of paper. On receiving a tip, the man fetched the items and left him to pen his message, leaning across a barrel in the corner.

A RELUCTANT HERO

Whereupon, once the ink was dry, he returned to Hawkins and handed him the note.

And a short time later they parted, Lord Ballater's servant to complete his errand and Revill to take himself to another part of the town, where he would make his plans.

By now, he had a suspicion who the failed fire-raiser – or fire-raisers – might be; and rightly or wrongly, he intended to find out.

***

The rest of the day passed quietly enough. Revill bought a pie from a bakery, then wandered to the north-western part of the city, where he found a pleasant green shaded by trees. Here he sat down to wait, until the sun was sinking and a small crowd of people came riding in through the west gate, talking in animated fashion. Many were well-dressed city officials, who had spent time with the Queen's party at Stansted Park. A few stragglers followed on foot, thinning out until the Minster bells clanged for evensong. At which point Revill got up, dusted off his breeches and walked over to the north wall of the great church. Here, at this hour, he had asked Shearer to meet him. He could only hope that the man was able to get away without any trouble.

To his relief, he did not have long to wait. A short time later his fellow-infiltrator in Lord Ballater's company appeared, walking quickly towards him. He wore his sword, and a hat pulled low. Revill stepped out into the street to greet him.

'Did you concoct a tale?' He asked. 'I hope it was better than the one I tried to fashion.'

Shearer gave a shrug. 'His Lordship's taken to his bed since noon. He needs to rest, Harman says. So does poor old Bridges… the shock of what happened has hit him hard. Given that all was calm, I said I needed to go out for a while. Nobody tried to stop me.'

'And Hawkins?'

'There's a change in him, I'd say. Since the fire, and what followed, he sees you and me differently. In short, he'd stand by us – especially you.'

'Let's hope it won't come to that,' Revill said.

'But what will you do now?' Shearer enquired, his brow creasing. 'You want me to get word to Cecil, or-'

'I want you to help me deal with Hooper, and possibly Godwin too.'

A moment passed. 'Ah... you've been doing some thinking, have you?'

'Shall we take a walk?' Revill suggested, pointing. 'The sward over there's quiet enough.'

In step, with heads lowered, the two of them crossed the west-gate road. Passers-by were few: young couples walking hand-in-hand and latecomers to church, none of whom paid any mind to two gentlemen enjoying an evening stroll. But by the time they had taken a turn about the green, Revill had laid forth his views about the fire that had come close to killing them both, and about who was behind it. Finally, Shearer stopped and turned to face him.

'A second attempt to silence you, like the one at Cowdray?' A pained look appeared. 'And you think Hooper's involved? What about Heneage, and his little toad Bryant?'

'I believe it's all of a piece,' Revill replied. 'A nest of thieves. Heneage knows I'm here, and I'd wager Bryant blurted everything out after I questioned him. Who else has such a need to snuff me out? And Hooper works for him, in his grubby scheme to profit from the Crown Purchases... likely Godwin does too.'

'But why go to such lengths?' Shearer asked. 'Wouldn't Heneage send some varlet to catch you in the dark, like before?' He paused. 'And what of me? Was my death desired too?'

'It would make it look more like an accident, would it not? No matter how clumsy the attempt was. Then, I suspect none of Heneage's people have much skill as fire-starters.'

'And yet, someone arranged to get Hawkins out of danger cleanly enough,' Shearer said.

'Someone did.'

Falling silent, Revill gazed towards the city wall and the hills beyond, bathed in the warm glow of sunset. Hawkins' account of being distracted by the woman called Margaret, lured to a low tavern and then drugged, troubled him. Why, he wondered, would

A RELUCTANT HERO

Heneage's people want to do that? He did not believe that Hawkins was lying, and yet…

'By the Christ, I'm muddled by all of this,' Shearer said suddenly, breaking his thoughts. 'We need to tell Cecil, and quickly. He has the power to act – and he has the ear of the Queen too. But in the meantime…' He waited for Revill to meet his eye, then: 'I'm uneasy about haring off to find Hooper just to pay him out, as you seem inclined. Things might go awry – we could both end up with our heads in the noose.'

'We could,' Revill agreed. 'But I confess I'm a little resentful of men trying to burn me to death… me, and one I regard as a friend too.'

Shearer drew a breath, but said nothing.

'Or,' Revill continued, 'we could overpower Hooper and haul him off to Stansted, to make his confession before the Queen's Council. I'd like to see Heneage's face, wouldn't you?'

'And your friend Godwin?' Shearer enquired, after a pause.

'I'm willing to keep my mind open about him,' Revill said. 'But just now, he's useful. In short, he's the one who can point us to Hooper, wherever he is.'

'You mean, you know where Godwin is?'

'Just a notion,' Revill answered. 'I shared a chamber with him, remember.' He raised his brows. 'So – are you coming with me, or not?'

***

The low tavern by the Greyfriars was, as Revill already suspected, more than merely an alehouse: it was a bawdy-house. And the kitchen maid - seemingly someone's friend, who helped out on occasions at Hugh Bridges' house for spare money – was a trull who had been paid to entice Hawkins away for the night. Hence, knowing Nicholas Godwin as he did, he had a notion that this was one place to start. Failing that, he would enquire as to the locations of other such premises about the city, and search them all until he found his man.

He had grown angry: a soldier's smouldering anger, directed towards any man who had tried to take his life by treachery. And just now, he was resolved to have justice.

His first port of call, however, looked like being a disappointment.

The house was, as Hawkins had said, a grimy little place, the drinkers an ill-favoured lot. Suspicious looks appeared as Revill and Shearer walked in, armed and alert... but for the whoremaster, they presented an opportunity. At once a swarthy-looking man in a pinked leather jerkin appeared, greeted them eagerly and asked if they were looking for company. But when Revill asked after the woman known as Margaret, his grin faded slightly.

'Not here tonight, sir. But it's no matter, for I've two other fair maids ready to serve you. Will you walk upstairs?'

'The matter is,' Revill said, 'it's Margaret I wanted to see. She vowed to meet a friend of mine last night, only she never came. Instead, something got put in his drink, and he's none too pleased about it. Nor am I, come to that.'

There was a pause, as the man stiffened visibly. After glancing at Shearer, who regarded him coolly, he looked away quickly. But before he could form a reply, Revill leaned closer to him and followed through.

'No need to wet yourself,' he said, speaking low. 'I'm not the law, and how a fellow does business is his own affair. It's not Margaret I'm seeking, but someone she might know – likely you know him too. If he hasn't been here of late, I'd wager he's at another trugging-house in this town. If you'll point me to him, there's a sixpence for you.'

Another moment passed. The pander – as seedy a rogue as Revill had set eyes on in a long while – glanced about uneasily. But then, the offer of a fee was not to be spurned.

'Does this man have a name?' He asked. And when Revill told him, a look of recognition appeared. 'Godwin? Well now, I believe I can send you to where he might be, though I can't swear to it. Are you content?'

With that, he held out a hand and waited. And a few moments later, poorer by sixpence, Revill left the premises with Shearer close behind.

Their destination now was a grander establishment, in a private house close by Chichester's north gate. Godwin, it transpired, had visited the low tavern by the Greyfriars only once, and thought little of it. But for a small remuneration, the pander had recommended a place run by a woman of his acquaintance, who could provide the gentleman with whatever he wished.

The woman's name was Eleanor Fiske; and the maid Margaret, who sometimes worked as a kitchen wench in the houses of the gentry, was her daughter.

TEN

By the time Revill and Shearer arrived at the house of Mistress Fiske, night had fallen. The walk took only ten minutes, but it was long enough for the two of them to form a strategy for dealing with Nicholas Godwin – provided he could be found. If not, Revill would have to find other means to track the man down. He even considered riding out to Stansted Park and asking for the whereabouts of the Crown Purveyors, before dismissing the notion as reckless. But a need was upon him, to discover whether Godwin or Hooper were involved in the attempt to murder him. What might follow after that, he was uncertain.

As fortune would have it, the search would end not long after he and Shearer had been admitted to the house, to enter a well-furnished parlour. At once, the owner rose from an alcove at the rear and came forward to greet them.

'Good Christ,' Shearer muttered under his breath. 'She looks like a duchess.'

Eleanor Fiske was indeed a handsome woman, a little above forty years of age, elegantly dressed in a sea-green gown embroidered with blue and silver. The hair was neatly-coiffed, the jewels at her ears and neck glittering in the candlelight. This was someone who served the better-off clients of the city, secure in the knowledge of the position that gave her. For a moment, Revill was half-inclined to give an ironic bow. There was time to observe the house's door-keeper – a huge man, poised to step forward should need arise – before he summoned a smile and returned the greeting.

'I'm here on recommendation of your daughter, madam,' he said. 'Margaret, is it not?'

'That is her name, sir,' the woman replied, her smile intact. 'Though she's absent just now. Will you and your friend take a drink of sack, before we talk of other matters?'

A RELUCTANT HERO

Revill turned to Shearer, who gave a nod; it seemed expedient. The two of them were shown to a table in the alcove, where a young maid in a very low-cut taffeta gown appeared with a jug. As they took their seats, wine was poured into chased silver cups.

'I must ask you to lay aside your swords, sirs,' the maid said. 'It's house custom.'

Revill nodded, aware that he was being watched by the giant beside the door. He and Shearer stood to unbuckle and handed the weapons to the girl. As they did so, Eleanor Fiske came to join them.

'I've not had the pleasure of seeing you before, gentles,' she began, as they sat down. 'Are you here to follow the Queen's train, as so many are?'

'In a way,' Revill answered. 'And in truth, we have but a short time before we must return to our place.' With that he turned to Shearer, who spoke as they had arranged.

'We're Crown Purchasers, madam,' he said. 'I understand you've already entertained a good friend of ours... Master Godwin? He speaks highly of you – and of your ladies.'

There was a pause as Mistress Fiske met his eye, then glanced at Revill. For a moment it seemed as if the statement had displeased her... until her next words brought relief.

'How kind,' the woman said, inclining her head. 'I had no notion until recently how many men of your sort attended the Queen. Then I heard that the harbingers who rode ahead of her train numbered ten at least – quite a company. Hence, I suppose a small flock of Purveyors should be no surprise. And Master Godwin has indeed visited us.'

'Has he been here to-day?' Revill asked, raising his brows.

This time, the question was unwelcome. They had arrived as men seeking the company of women, and were expected to talk business. Instead of replying, Mistress Fiske took up her cup, sipped and lowered it again.

'In truth, sir, it's not my habit to speak of who is here or who is not,' she said. 'Would you like to see portraits of my girls now? I can promise you a most pleasurable time.'

'Perhaps I should explain,' Revill said. 'It's Godwin I'm seeking – a private matter between the two of us. If you will aid me, I'll pay what I would have spent for a night with one of your maids. Then we'll be gone.'

At that a silence fell, profound enough for both men to become aware of sounds from above: a rhythmic thudding, accompanied by faint cries of pleasure. Across the room, Mistress Fiske's muscular guardian remained alert for a signal.

'Pray, what is this private matter?' She enquired.

'It's merely business - of mutual interest,' Revill replied. 'Speaking of which, would you care to name a price? Provided you can aid us, that is.'

'Your pardon, but I'm loth to do so,' the pander said. 'I'm known for my discretion... customers put their trust in me. For all I know-'

'Tell me, what price for your best girl?' Shearer broke in. 'As much as a crown? We'll pay it, and you'll not see us again. Nor will we speak of how we learned of Godwin's whereabouts. And I too, madam, am known for my discretion.'

With that he put on a smile that, Revill had to admit, would have charmed a duchess. And to his satisfaction, Mistress Fiske relented.

'I would like your promise that no violent behaviour is to be offered,' she said flatly. Her gracious manner had vanished; this was business now, pure and simple.

'You have it,' Revill said, his face impassive.

'Moreover, I insist on accompanying you.'

For a moment neither of the men understood – and then the penny dropped.

'You mean, he's here now?' Revill said, allowing his gaze to shift to the ceiling.

For answer Mistress Fiske merely rose, threw a glance at her door-keeper, then gestured towards a stairway. In stately fashion, she led the way up to the landing and stopped at the first door. Without knocking she opened it, to be greeted by startled voices, male and female.

A RELUCTANT HERO

'Wait here,' she said shortly. Then she was inside, issuing terse instructions. A moment later a very young woman appeared, clutching a shift to cover her nakedness, and stumbled into the passage. With a hard look at the two men, she hurried off to disappear through another door. Whereupon the lady of the house emerged, to face Revill.

'I'll have the payment now,' she said. 'Then you must take your friend away, and conduct your business elsewhere. And,' she added, with a glance at each of them in turn, 'I mean to hold you to your promise.'

With that, she waited until Revill had produced his purse and handed over a crown. Then she was gone, walking unhurriedly towards the stairhead. With a glance at each other, the two of them entered the room – to find Nicholas Godwin on his feet, struggling into his breeches and wearing a look of alarm.

'By God – you!' He cried. 'What the devil…?'

'I'd like a talk,' Revill said. 'Outside, I mean. When you're ready?'

***

They marched Godwin between them, away from the house and through the streets, round the city wall to the green where Revill had spent much of the day. Here, beneath the sprawling branches of a great oak, they stopped. Thus far, since leaving Eleanor Fiske's premises under the watchful eye of the giant on the door, neither he nor Shearer had spoken. Godwin, however, had begun protesting from the moment they were outdoors. This was intolerable, he had said repeatedly; he would report them, have them arrested… had they forgotten who he was? But since neither man paid him any attention, he had gradually lapsed into silence. Now, eyeing them both warily, he stood in the gloom with his back to the tree. Revill and Shearer had both recovered their swords from Mistress Fiske's before leaving, but had somehow neglected to allow Godwin to retrieve his.

'Why not sit and be comfortable?' Revill invited. 'It's dry, and we may be here for a while.'

Godwin, however, made no move to comply. He was frightened, but he was angry too.

'You can't do this,' he blurted. 'Whatever your charge against me – and in God's name, I can't think what it could be – then lay it forth, and let's cease this nonsense!'

But for answer Revill merely shoved him, forcing him into a sitting position. For a moment, he thought fleetingly, he was back in the wood at Cowdray, interrogating a terrified Bryant... drawing a breath, he looked down at his new victim.

'So, who set the fire at Bridges' house?' He enquired. 'You, or Hooper, or someone else?'

'What?' Godwin stared. 'For Christ's sake-'

'Don't take us for fools,' Shearer said, moving forward; they had chosen their roles, and his was that of hard inquisitor. 'You're already in difficulties, so spill your tale.'

'What tale?' The other adopted a bewildered look. 'You know me, and what I do,' he said, facing Revill. 'I may not be a saint, but I'm no fire-setter either. It's absurd!'

'Last night, someone tried to burn the building where we both slept,' Shearer snapped. 'We could have died – which was doubtless the intent. We know who your associates are, as we know why my friend here is deemed a threat. Do you understand now?'

'No, I don't!' Godwin retorted, growing flushed. 'And I can't see-'

'Heneage,' Revill broke in. 'Sir Thomas of that name, Vice-Chamberlain to the Queen and in charge of supplies for her Progress. You and Hooper do what he wants you to, and get a sweet payment in return. His secretary Bryant admitted it, so let's not waste time, eh?'

'Bryant?' Godwin echoed. 'You can't believe what that little weasel says. He'd swear anything to save his neck!'

'Is that what you mean to do?' Shearer demanded. 'In which case, it won't work.' He laid a hand on his sword-hilt, making the man flinch.

'Will you listen to me?' He cried. 'I don't... I mean, it isn't as you think...'

A RELUCTANT HERO

'How odd,' Revill put in. 'Those were almost the words Bryant used, just before someone shot me. First a pistol, then attempted arson... it smacks of desperation, does it not?'

'Mayhap it does!' Godwin threw back. 'But either way, the two of you seem to have lost your heads...' He broke off, and drew a breath. 'See now,' he added. 'I'll allow there are... there might have been some irregularities in what I do, but-'

'Irregularities?' Shearer gave a snort. 'You're a thief, Godwin. And when word of it reaches the ears of the Queen's Councillors, then-'

'Then the law of the Verge applies,' Revill finished. 'You'll be for the gallows, Master Purveyor. You and your friend Hooper - and Heneage too, if I had my way. Unless...' He raised his brows. 'Unless there's anything else you'd care to tell us?'

'Listen, you can't go throwing accusations at a man like Heneage,' Godwin said, his gaze flitting nervously between the two of them. 'You don't know him, or what-'

'Oh, but I do,' Revill said broke in. 'Better than you can imagine. But in any case, I suspect this Progress will be his last. It will certainly be yours.'

A moment passed. Thus far Revill and Shearer had remained calm, and it had paid off: Godwin saw their resolve, and dropped his gaze. His customary swagger had ebbed away, to leave a frightened man who had begun to see that the game was over... and on a sudden, he wilted. Sitting back against the bole of the great oak, he put a hand to his forehead and let out a sigh.

'See now, I've a wife and three brats back in London,' he muttered, looking up. 'Do you think men like me are well-rewarded? What would you have done when good money can be had - crowns, instead of the miserable shillings I'm paid? Would you have spurned the offer? I'll wager my last penny you wouldn't.'

His answer was a cold silence.

'And I had debts too,' Godwin persisted. 'When you owe money to a man like Hooper...' he drew a breath. 'You've crossed swords with him yourself – you've seen what he's like.'

'So, it was he who arranged the fire,' Revill said.

'I swear to God I don't know!' Came the angry reply. 'He takes his orders from Heneage – they tell me nothing.' He paused, then: 'I know Hooper wants you dead, but...' he gave a shrug. 'There's another man, the one you saw at Dell's Quay. He's a varlet through and through, but he's Hooper's varlet. Not the cleverest of fellows – and by the sound of it he made a poor fist of fire-setting, if that's what he was sent to do. For here you are - and here I am, at your mercy. So for pity's sake, tell me what you mean to do!'

'You have a wife, you say?' Revill murmured, after a moment. And when the other gave a nod: 'She must be a very patient woman.'

'She isn't at all,' Godwin said, looking away. 'But she's a good mother to the brats.'

'A shame about their father,' Shearer put in scornfully.

'That varlet, as you call him, whom I saw at the quay,' Revill said. 'What's his name?'

'Walden... Miles Walden.'

'And where will I find him, and Hooper?'

'At Stansted...' Godwin frowned. 'You're not going there? They'd kill you!'

'Where at Stansted?' Revill continued, as if he hadn't heard. 'Surely not in the big house?'

'Of course not. There are cottages on the edge of the park, where huntsmen and falconers live with their families. The Purveyors are lodged in the end one.' Godwin eyed him. 'But see now,' he added nervously, 'what about me?'

'You?' Revill eyed him, threw a glance at Shearer, then returned his gaze to their hapless informant. 'As my friend said, you're a thief. You should be in Newgate – or even dangling from Tyburn Tree. But then, we're not the law... and you've a family, you say. So, what can I do but let you return to them, and forget I ever saw you?'

For a moment, Godwin didn't understand. Then, when both Revill and Shearer turned their backs, he let out a gasp and scrambled to his feet. There followed a brief sound of footsteps, fading rapidly in the distance.

A RELUCTANT HERO

'You let him off too lightly,' Shearer said. And when Revill made no answer: 'But the night draws on, and I should get back to His Lordship.'

'Of course...' Revill faced him. 'Once again, you have my thanks.'

'You know that Cecil must be told of this – and soon.'

'Can I leave that to you?'

The other gave a nod. 'But see now, what will you do? You can't act alone.'

'What choice do I have?' Revill shrugged. 'I'm a solitary player... one of those who waits until the others leave the stage, then spouts some speech about honour, or glory-'

'Or death,' Shearer finished.

'Goodman Death and I are old adversaries,' Revill answered, with a hint of a smile. 'But I don't intend to challenge him again, just yet. I'll find a way.'

'I thought you might say that,' his companion said, with a sigh. 'In which case, you leave me too without a choice. Have you forgotten why Cecil got me into Ballater's service?'

'You've done a great deal already,' Revill told him. 'Meanwhile, there's still the matter of His Lordship's plot, even if I don't believe it exists. Someone has to keep watch.'

For a moment they stood in silence, then Shearer clapped him suddenly on the shoulder.

'I forgot to tell you. Ballater intends to ride over to Stansted tomorrow evening to present his petition to the Queen. If he's admitted to her presence, that is. The old fool may be deluding himself, but...' he grew brisk. 'You could follow us – from a discreet distance, of course. Then I'll slip away and meet you... will that serve?'

Revill met his eye, and relaxed.

***

Evening on the following day found him beside Malachi, overlooking the road leading westward from Chichester.

It had been a long day, and he was restless. He had spent the night in an inn, then most of the day riding the surrounding countryside. But at last, having scouted the edges of Stansted Park and seen the big house in the distance, he had picked his spot and was ready. Concealed behind a clump of bushes, he held the horse's rein and watched. People had been passing for some hours, riding to and from Lord Lumley's residence, but the road was now quiet. And as yet, there was no sign of Lord Ballater or his servants.

By now, Revill had had more than enough time to mull over his plans, and to realise how reckless they were. It was quite likely that he would find Hooper, and his henchman Walden too – but what then? Even with Shearer beside him, he was set for a difficult encounter. The memory of getting the better of Hooper, back at the Woolpack in Steadham, brought little encouragement. He was recalling the man on the ground, bleeding and spitting angry words, when the sound of hoofbeats shook him from his reverie.

Peering above the bushes, he saw riders approaching – and there was no mistaking their identity.

Harman rode first, at a modest pace. Then came the familiar figure of His Lordship on his stout horse, wearing his best attire topped with hat and riding cloak. Behind him Hawkins and Shearer were riding together, stirrup to stirrup. Soon they would draw level with Revill's vantage-point... crouching, he reached up to pat Malachi's neck and murmured a few words, which the old warhorse understood well enough. They remained still until the party had moved past, hoofbeats fading. Whereupon, after judging the moment Revill stood up, mounted quickly and eased the horse out into the road, to follow from a distance.

It was only three miles to Stansted, but by the time he had arrived the light was already fading, which was a blessing. In the distance, music drifted from the house, and on the wide lawn before it figures moved back and forth in the glow of torches set out on stands. Backing Malachi into the shelter of some broad-leafed trees, Revill dismounted and tethered him to a branch. Then he was moving forward on foot, seeking the dwellings Shearer had spoken of.

It took longer than he expected. From the description he knew that the cottages stood on a shallow-sloping hillside, facing the hunting fields. Set apart from them was a falcon's mews, where

A RELUCTANT HERO

they were to meet as soon as Shearer could get away. It would be quiet at this time, the birds having been settled for the night. The cottages, however, would be occupied - and the proximity of the wives and children of Lord Lumley's men troubled him. Somehow, he must accost Hooper and get him away to question him; if the man Walden proved an obstacle, he would have to be silenced. But then, if it were he who had set the fire at the outhouse as Godwin seemed to think, Revill had little sympathy for him - and few scruples about how to quiet him.

Moving through long grass, on a sudden he felt the ground slope away beneath his boots - and stopped in his tracks. Before him dark shapes appeared, hugging the hillside. He had stumbled directly upon the cottages, almost close enough to hear sounds from within.

Instinctively he dropped to a crouch, peering about. A light showed at the window of the nearest cottage, which was in truth little more than a hut. There were four of them, thatched and fenced off with a row of withies. But further off, to his right, he glimpsed the mews: a low, circular structure. Within seconds he had moved soundlessly towards it, rounded it to the side facing away from the dwellings, and taken his position.

Mercifully, he had only a half hour to wait before footsteps came swishing through the grass, followed by a low whistle. He returned the signal, and was relieved to see Shearer loom out of the gathering dusk. And without preamble, the man delivered his tidings.

'Ballater,' he breathed, squatting down beside Revill. 'The Queen won't see him... her Councillors sent him away with his tail between his legs.'

'Isn't that to the good?' Revill said, after taking in the news. 'He can't cause any mischief now, can he? If he ever intended it-'

'Listen,' Shearer broke in. 'The Progress is leaving either tomorrow or the day after, but His Lordship intends to follow it anyway. He's got it into his head that the Queen's teasing him – making him dance attendance at her pleasure. He'll return to Bridges' house tonight, pack up and be ready to leave. So you see,

I'm expected back. I've stolen a few minutes while the others are taking a drink, but...'

He broke off with a shrug, for the implications were clear. In the gloom, the two of them were silent for a moment – until Revill formed his resolve.

'You should return, and do as Cecil ordered.'

'What about you?'

'I'll survive.'

'You're certain of that, are you?'

In the twilight, Revill grinned. 'Of course... I'm famous for my luck, or so I'm told.'

'Then, what can I do but wish you God speed?' Came the reply. A hand came up to grasp his... only to be followed by a sudden oath.

'Oh, to the devil with Ballater!' Shearer exclaimed. 'Let him ride back without me... I can make my excuses later.' A pause, then: 'Did you really think I'd let you face those rogues alone?'

Whereupon they both stood up, to turn their attention to the cottage at the end of the row.

A RELUCTANT HERO

ELEVEN

The hut – the smallest and meanest of the dwellings – faced away from the others, shaded by a large tree. There was but one storey, probably with a sleeping loft above. As Revill and Shearer climbed over the fence they heard sounds from within, and saw a glow of lanternlight. Then they were at the door, with a shuttered window to their left.

There had been little time to form a plan. Shearer was armed with sword and poniard, and had had the foresight to bring a pistol, concealed under his jerkin. Revill had only his sword, having yet to replace the poniard he had broken back at the outhouse. But he had faced worse odds, and this was no time to dwell on the risks. When Shearer tapped him on the arm and moved aside, he stood up squarely before the door, and knocked.

What he heard next was unexpected: a peal of laughter, followed by a raucous voice calling out what sounded like 'I win!' The next moment, someone was on the other side of the door.

'There's no lock, you whoreson clod!' The occupant shouted. 'Have you forgotten? Get your sorry arse in here, and give account of yourself!'

For a moment Revill hesitated – until what followed made matters clearer.

'Godwin! What in blazes are you about? Come in, damn you!'

It was Hooper's voice… and he sounded rather drunk. Drawing a breath, Revill put his hand to the latch, lifted it and thrust the door wide.

'Good evening,' he said.

The result was a stunned silence. Hooper, in shirt sleeves, stared at him in disbelief. In his hand was a leather mug, of the kind used by horsemen. So taken aback was he that he let it fall, spilling liquid on the floor. Meanwhile another figure came up, to peer over his shoulder.

'Who the devil... wait, I've eyed you before, have I not?' It was Walden, whom he had first seen on horseback at Dell's Quay. And as he spoke, Hooper frowned.

'By God, you've got some sinew,' he began – only to break off with a start, as Shearer stepped smartly into view with his pistol levelled. Both purveyors drew back at once.

'May we come in?' Shearer asked. Upon which he and Revill crossed the threshold, forcing the others to retreat before them. Soon they were backed against the rear wall of what was revealed to be a very humble, dim-lit dwelling, cluttered with assorted baggage. On an upturned keg nearby was a dice-shaker, with dice and several coins.

Allowing Shearer to move past him, Revill turned and closed the door quietly.

'Good Christ, what do you want?'

Hooper was scowling. Beside him, Walden looked warily at the intruders. Like his companion he was unarmed, in loose clothing, and somewhat the worse for drink. Clearly the two of them had been doing some celebrating.

'Let's start by talking of the fire you tried to set,' Revill suggested. 'Somewhat ham-fisted, was it not? Moreover, I'd say you owe the gentleman who owns the building a tidy sum in reparations.'

'I asked what you wanted,' Hooper said, trying to sound confident. Unfortunately, he failed. Finding himself faced with the man who had beaten him easily in a sword-bout – and who now looked bent on some sort of revenge - he was unnerved.

'So, you thought I was Godwin,' Revill pressed on. 'Your pardon for the disappointment, but you won't see him again.'

At that both men stiffened, whereupon Shearer, who was still pointing the pistol, added his contribution. 'Poor fellow,' he said, putting on a sad expression. 'Him with a wife and children, too. How will they fadge, I wonder?'

'Jesus...' Hooper swallowed. 'Listen, whatever Godwin told you, he was lying. A louse and a weakling, who-'

'Who would swear anything to save his neck?' Revill broke in. 'How odd – that's what he said about Bryant. Heneage certainly picks his men, does he not? I speak of the Queen's Vice-Chamberlain, your master in falsehood – and in felony too.'

Another taut silence followed, while the two exchanged looks. Desperation made men reckless... Revill recalled thinking something like that, the last time he and Hooper were at loggerheads. On impulse he put his hand to his sword-hilt, making both him and Walden flinch... then came a surprise.

'Bryant's gone,' Walden said, in a surly tone. 'He was dismissed.'

'Well then,' Revill said, after a pause. 'That leaves just the two of you.'

'Perhaps it does.' The man met his eye, as if to convey meaning. He was the braver of the two, Revill decided, and he was calculating his next move. Whereupon, somewhat quickly, Hooper spoke.

'It doesn't have to fall out this way, Perrot – do you not see that?'

As one, Revill and Shearer turned to him.

'Bryant's finished,' he went on, speaking quickly. 'And now you say Godwin's dead, so–'

'Did I say that?' Revill raised his eyebrows. 'I don't recall it.'

'You said I wouldn't see him again,' Hooper replied sharply. 'What game do you play?'

'No games,' Revill answered. 'Instead, I've a mind to arrest you. I'll swear out a warrant later... as a former captain of London trained-bands, I believe I have some authority.'

'You what?' Walden was glowering, fists clenched at his sides. 'You can go to hades!'

'Not so loud, my friend,' Shearer warned, levelling his pistol at the man's head. 'We don't want to frighten the neighbours, do we?'

'Will you listen to me, for pity's sake?' Hooper took a pace forward, throwing a glance at Walden to silence him. 'I was about to offer terms, if you'll hear them,' he added. 'Or would you rather remain a servant to Ballater? What does that old keg of lard pay you? Think! I could offer you as much in a day as you'd earn in a month–'

'That's enough!' In a voice of ice, Revill silenced him. 'I'm done listening to your wheedling. For the last time, I'll ask which one of you tried to burn down the place where we lodged – and who gave the order. Tell me!'

A moment passed... whereupon, quite suddenly, matters turned.

'I've been looking at your wheel-lock,' Walden said, fixing his gaze on Shearer. 'Wondering if it was loaded - or even primed.'

'Are you sure you want to find out?' Shearer asked, his voice tight.

Revill had stiffened, his hand on his sword. Hooper stiffened too, his eyes darting about... but Walden remained motionless. Summoning a bland smile, he spread his hands as if in submission - and then he leaped.

But not at Shearer: he leaped aside, to where a sword hung from a nail in the wall. And as Hooper ducked aside, he seized it and yanked it from the scabbard. At the same moment Revill drew his rapier, while Shearer, whose empty pistol had failed to convince, dropped the firearm - and in seconds, mayhem broke out.

It was short, but bloody.

Four swordsmen in a tight, cluttered space... or rather three with swords, since Hooper had seemingly mislaid his. Wherever it was, he had no time to retrieve it. Revill stepped out of Shearer's way, allowing him space to meet his assailant. Then he was upon Hooper, dealing him a crack to the jaw that sent him reeling. He fell on his back among some saddle-bags, all of them seemingly well-stuffed – and froze, as the tip of Revill's rapier was put to his wind-pipe. In falling he had tried to catch the lantern which hung from a beam overhead, but failed to grasp it. It now swung wildly, casting a flickering light over the drama; had he reached it, Revill thought briefly, another fire might have started – one that could have been the end of all of them. But even as the thought passed, there came a cry of agony from close by. Keeping his sword-point at his victim's throat, he glanced aside... and breathed a sigh of relief: Walden had lost the bout already.

But then, he had never stood a chance against Shearer. Moreover, like Hooper he was somewhat clumsy from whatever drink he had taken. Without attempting to wield his sword in the cramped cottage, Shearer had simply drawn his preferred weapon: the poniard, with which he had slain Revill's attacker back in the wood at Cowdray. When Walden lunged at him, he had dashed his opponent's rapier aside with his forearm and brought the dagger up swiftly, thrusting it hard between his ribs. Now he drew back, withdrew the blade and stood as the man crumpled to the floor.

'By God... God in heaven...'

It was Hooper, turning his head slightly to see his companion fall, blood welling from the wound. Thereafter the three survivors watched him die without a sound: a rapid paling of the flesh above the heavy beard, an empty look in the eyes... a final breath, and he was gone.

With a sigh, Shearer dropped his weapon. At the same moment, a noise from outside startled them: the barking of a large hound. The neighbours, of course; it was sheer luck that no dog had sensed the intruders' presence already.

'On your feet – now!'

Removing his blade from Hooper's throat, Revill snapped out the order. And even as the other began to rise, there came a rap on the door. A male voice called out, but the words were indistinct.

'Hurry yourself,' Revill said. 'Go to the door, open it a few inches and tell him all's well in here. A bit of horseplay, nothing more - do it!'

Hooper got to his feet; he was shaken, a sickly look on his features. Watched closely by the other two, he moved towards the door while Shearer stepped clear. Revill, however, sheathed his rapier quickly, stooped to pick up Shearer's dagger and pressed it to Hooper's spine.

'One word out of place and I'll use it,' he murmured. 'And I don't bluff.'

Mercifully, the matter was dealt with easily enough. While Revill remained out of sight, pressed to the wall, Hooper opened the door slightly and spoke a greeting. Words passed between him and the unseen visitor, who was clearly holding the dog: there came a low growl, followed by a word of command which silenced the animal. Thereafter, Hooper's muttered explanation served its purpose, and with a curt good-night he closed the door. Then he turned slowly, his face haggard.

'What'll you do now – kill me, or arrest me like you said?' He muttered, without looking up. 'For either way, the result will be the same.'

'That's true enough.'

It was Shearer, gathering himself after those last, desperate moments. Moving forward, he grasped Hooper by the shoulder and shoved him across the room, towards the wall where he had stood earlier. Revill moved too, letting the blood-stained poniard fall to the floor. On a sudden they were interrogators again, as they had interrogated the hapless Godwin only the evening before.

'First, tell me about Heneage,' Revill said, calmly enough.

A pause followed, then: 'Such as what?'

'Such as, was it he who gave the order to have me killed?'

The other paused, then let out a sigh; with Walden's death, the fight seemed to have gone out of him. Finally, he gave a nod.

'Was it this one who set the fire?' Revill gestured briefly towards the body. 'I'm unsure, but for some reason I think you'd have made a better job of it.'

Another nod followed.

'And was it you who arranged for our chamber-fellow to be absent, and out of danger?'

At that, Hooper lifted his gaze. 'What chamber-fellow?'

'Hawkins, who was led astray by a trull – one of Godwin's pieces of laced mutton,' Shearer put in harshly. 'We know what happened.'

'Then you know more than I,' Hooper mumbled, with a shake of his head. 'I don't keep count of Godwin's whores... mayhap you should have asked him.'

The others made no reply. But watching the man, Revill believed he was speaking the truth - and hence, this was one matter as yet unexplained. He was forming another question when Hooper spoke up again.

'I asked what you're going to do,' he said bitterly. 'You've despatched Godwin and... him.' This, with a jerk of his thumb towards his late companion. 'So why do you wait?'

'I'm thinking on it,' Revill told him. 'Meanwhile, tell me more about Heneage. Is he enjoying the Progress? Is he by the Queen's side much? How's his standing these days, among the rest of her Council?'

'Are you jesting with me?' Hooper looked pained. 'How would I know such-'

'You're his lieutenant,' Shearer broke in. 'The master of his tawdry little game. What were the others, but foot-soldiers? Speak up!'

'All right, damn you!' On a sudden, a wild look appeared on their captive's face. 'What is it you want to hear?' He cried. 'That Heneage is desperate? That he's sinking under a hill of debt, fighting with his daughter and her snake of a husband? That he's jealous of Cecil, and knows he's being edged aside for the younger man? Or do you want to hear that he's in pain half the time, and snapping at anyone within earshot? Will that satisfy you?'

He fell silent then, sagging like an emptied sack. And while the other two regarded him in some surprise, he slumped to the floor and fell back against the wall. Finally, Revill spoke.

'I believe it's time to disobey orders,' he said, turning to Shearer. 'If you'll go and break the news to our superior, I'll take charge of the prisoner. The matter's somewhat beyond our warrant now, is it not?'

Shearer let out a breath, and signalled agreement.

***

An hour later, in a quiet corner of Stansted's spacious gardens, the meeting took place in semi-darkness.

This night Sir Robert Cecil presented a somewhat different persona to Revill, since they had last met in the crowded kitchen at West Dean. In full courtier mode, with a new suit of black silk and a rapier with a jewelled hilt, he was impatient at having been brought away from the Queen's company. Meanwhile, from the great house, the sounds of music and revelry persisted. By now Shearer had given the Councillor a brief but full account of what had occurred. And a short distance away, in the shadows, sat Hooper, his wrists and ankles tied before him and a gag about his mouth. Cecil took one look at the prisoner, then faced Revill.

'I seem to recall I warned you before, about straying from your purpose,' he said. 'Now you appear to have appointed yourself sergeant-at-arms... and you too,' he added, with a wry look at Shearer. 'What in God's name possessed you?'

'We've laid bare a conspiracy, Sir Robert,' Shearer said, managing to conceal his indignation. 'We didn't plan to end up here... in truth, we're lucky to be alive to tell of it.'

'I see that,' Cecil replied sharply. But there was no real rancour; he was thinking fast, Revill saw. He recalled their first meeting in London, when he had begun to like the man.

'We thought you should know the whole of it without delay, sir,' he put in mildly. 'It's too grave a matter for us.' He allowed his glance to stray towards Hooper. Eyes on the ground, the man looked the very picture of defeat.

'Well, first things first,' Cecil said, growing brisk. 'Tomorrow, I'll send that one to London under guard, to await my return. As for Heneage...' He paused. 'You must forget about him. This is a Privy Council matter.'

The other two were silent.

'As for you...' He eyed Shearer. 'You should return to Chichester at once, excuse yourself to Lord Ballater and resume your duties. And don't leave his company again.'

Though dispirited by the notion, Shearer nodded. But he caught Revill's eye, and a current of understanding passed between them: they were brothers-in-arms now, either of whom would come to the other's aid without question. Thereafter, seeing that his master had nothing more to say he turned and walked off, to retrieve his horse and quit Stansted.

Revill would have spoken, but Cecil forestalled him.

'For now, you will join me here as one of my party,' he announced. 'A captain of trained-bands, newly come from London. And your first task is to bring that man in to Stansted.' He nodded towards Hooper, who was looking balefully at them both.

'Bring him in?' Revill echoed. 'You mean, as-'

'I mean as a thief, who was caught dipping where he shouldn't,' Cecil broke in. 'Lock him in the cellar, and make sure he can't speak to anyone. I'll send another man to help you. After that, you don't say another word about him - or about his fellow Crown Purveyors.' He paused, then added drily: 'Of whom, it seems there are now none left. I'll speak to Lord Chamberlain Hunsdon, who will arrange for others to take over their task.'

'The hut where the purveyors lodged, sir,' Revill said, gesturing vaguely in that direction. 'It's... something of a battlefield just now.'

'Then you'd best clear it up, and thoroughly - this very night,' came the reply. 'The man I send will aid you. His name's Gillan. I won't give instructions about disposing of the body – you're the ex-soldier, not me. All that anyone will learn here is that Hooper, Walden and Godwin have left the Queen's Progress for reasons best known to themselves, and have forfeited their posts. Is that clear enough for you?'

'Clear enough,' Revill answered. On a sudden he felt very tired - until a thought surfaced that shook him. From all this mayhem, a glimmer of hope had appeared... seizing the moment, he spoke up.

'Your pardon, sir... before I get to work?' And when Cecil gave the briefest of nods: 'Whatever the future may hold for Sir Thomas Heneage, may I remind you of what you said, when I first stood before you at Whitehall? That this would truly be the last time I was at his beck and call... that the burden would be lifted, and my sister freed from-'

'From harassment, or worse,' Cecil finished. 'You have no need to remind me.'

Revill waited.

'Well... for the present, I'll say nothing to that,' his superior continued. 'My powers are limited - and you know the risks Papists face.' He paused. 'But serve me well, and we'll speak again. Just now, you have things to attend to, do you not?'

'I thank you, Sir Robert,' Revill said. And since that seemed to end the matter, Cecil was about to walk back to the house when, to his irritation, Revill stayed him again.

'Sir... one final request, I pray.'

'In heaven's name, what is it now?'

'I would dearly like to bid good-bye to Thomas Perrot, for ever. If I'm your man newly come from London, I would like to be Will Revill again. Will you allow that?'

'Oh, for pity's sake.' With a gesture of dismissal, Cecil signalled assent. 'Use your proper name, if the other displeases you so much. Now I'd like to return to my duties as a member of the Queen's Privy Council - if you'll allow me?'

Whereupon, without further word the little hunchback turned and stalked off.

Revill breathed a sigh, and addressed himself to taking Hooper into his charge, as a thief who had committed a felony within the Verge. As the man had said himself, but an hour previously: whether or not either Shearer or Revill had slain him, his fate was the same.

Soon after the Queen's Progress had returned to London, the gibbet awaited him.

A RELUCTANT HERO

TWELVE

The next morning, after the deepest night's sleep he had known in days, Revill awoke to bright sunlight streaming through a casement, with no idea where he was. He had been so exhausted by the exertions of the previous day, he barely remembered getting to bed. But here he was, in a narrow chamber with a steep-sloping roof, on a pallet beside several other pallets, all of them empty. From somewhere below came the sounds of a large household, already up and busy, while songbirds cheeped outside and swallows swooped past the open window... whereupon, everything came back to him in a rush.

With a groan, he sat up. Now, he recalled marching a subdued Hooper to the house, bringing him in by a rear door and taking him down to the cellars to be placed under lock and key. To questions from the kitchen folk, Revill and his helper, Cecil's man Gillan, answered that the prisoner was a thief awaiting trial, and not to be approached. Thereafter, the two of them had gone outside to begin the grisly work of removing Walden's body from the hut.

Walden, it was believed, had no family, so disposing of him was less troublesome than it might have been. Together, Revill and Gillan had dug a pit as far from the house as they could carry the corpse, and laid it to rest without ceremony. His weapons were also placed in the grave, to be covered with earth and turves. The two tired men had then returned to the Purveyors' lodging and tidied the place as best they could. A bag of money was found: gold coins to the amount of more than fifty crowns, the proceeds of weeks of malpractice by the Crown Purveyors. Gillan had taken charge of that, to hand it to his master.

Daniel Gillan was a surprise. Revill had expected a man-at-arms, but the one sent to assist him was a scrawny little fellow, grey-haired and somewhat stooped. His appearance, however, was deceptive: the strength he showed in carrying out their orders was more than ample, and Revill had warmed to him. When all was done, the two of them had cleaned themselves and taken a drink of sack, before climbing exhaustedly to the attic chamber that was shared with other men.

Thinking on it now, he saw the previous night's events as a bad dream: one that he hoped never to repeat. On a sudden, he thought of Jenna and wondered if, when he saw her again, he would have good news to impart... or was he clutching at straws?

Restlessly, he rose... whereupon the door opened and Gillan walked in.

'I thought I'd let you sleep a while,' he murmured, peering at Revill from under grizzled eyebrows. 'You were so tuckered out by the time we came to bed, you went off in a trice. I took the liberty of removing your shoes.'

Revill looked down and saw that, apart from his feet, the rest of him was clothed.

'You have my thanks, Master Daniel,' he said.

'Don't trouble yourself,' the other replied. 'You'd best get out to the stables. Sir Robert's going hawking with the Queen, and wants you to join the escort. Though you should keep back, he says, and not speak to him - nor to anyone else, apart from me.'

An outsider, once again; Revill barely nodded.

And a short time later, without the benefit of a breakfast, he was retrieving Malachi from the Stansted stables and riding out to join the royal party... which allowed him his first sight of the Queen's host, Lord John Lumley.

Baron Lumley, once notorious for involvement in Catholic conspiracies, was another surprise. This soberly-dressed, thin-faced man, his reddish beard turning grey, had the air of a philosopher more than anything else. At sight of him, riding an old hunting horse, Revill recalled Hawkins' account of Lumley back at the inn in Chichester. Was this really the one-time firebrand, who had been imprisoned for his faith? Now, it seemed he had chosen a quiet and bookish life - and like Sir Anthony Browne at Cowdray, was as attentive a host to his Queen as could be imagined.

Much of this Revill learned from Gillan, as they rode together at the rear of the hawking party, along with a baggage cart which

A RELUCTANT HERO

held the ingredients for a mid-day meal in the park: a French custom that had crossed the Channel, and was known as *pique-nique*. To Revill, after the events of recent days, the procedure sounded so genteel, he felt like a ruffian at the feast.

'I'm used to eating outdoors,' he said. 'And in France too, as it happens, though I never heard it called that before.'

'The Queen likes to stop for a rest nowadays,' Gillan said. 'She's no longer young. In her fifty-eighth year... same age as Lord Lumley.'

'I see Sir Robert's keeping an eye on him,' Revill observed, eying the man in the distance. 'That, or they've become bosom friends.'

'I doubt that,' his companion replied, with a dour look. 'They're poles apart in the matter of religion. Did you know Lumley's first wife attended Queen Mary?'

'I didn't. And so, the lady with him is his second wife?'

'The Lady Elizabeth.' Gillan nodded.

Revill gazed ahead at the royal party, as they hawked in the open park. Their birds flew high overhead, stooping to take prey now and again. Somewhere in the middle of the group was The Queen, surrounded by her ladies and favourites. Falconers and servants milled about on foot, while the nobles and gentry rode easily on their fine hunting horses. Cecil, a keen hawking man, was fully engaged... but there was no sign of Sir Thomas Heneage.

On a sudden Revill thought of his one-time spymaster, and what he had learned of him since. He had known for years that Heneage was an unprincipled rogue, but what Hooper had revealed to him was a shock: the man's debts, his ill-health, the fear that he was slipping from royal favour. Even so, his activities with the corrupt Crown Purveyors had come as a surprise; it spoke of desperation, something he had never imagined in a man like Heneage. How Cecil would proceed with him, Revill did not know; *a Privy Council matter*, he had been told. He was mulling it over when he saw that Gillan had slowed his mount, and was looking aside.

'Who's this?' He muttered.

Aware of approaching hoofbeats, Revill followed his gaze... and gave a start. A figure came riding up whom he recognised at once: Lord Ballater's steward, Harman.

'It's time for us to do our office,' Gillan said, and received a nod in return. They were supposed to be a rear guard on the lookout for uninvited petitioners, or indeed anyone who came too close to the Queen. Quickly Revill urged Malachi forward, to block Harman's way. As he and Gillan drew near, the man reined in sharply.

'By the Christ!' He glowered at Revill. 'You're here, like a bad penny? I hoped I'd seen the last of you. Now I'd be obliged if you'd move aside.'

'We've orders to stop anyone who rides in the Park unbidden, sir,' Gillan said at once. 'I must ask who you are, and what's your business.'

'Who I am?' The steward turned with a sneer. 'Why don't you ask him?' He pointed at Revill, who returned his gaze without expression.

'This man's name is Harman,' he said. 'He serves Lord Ballater, who was lately refused an audience with the Queen – did you hear of that?'

'Well now, I believe I did.' Gillan eased his horse forward a pace. 'And I'll ask again, Master Harman: what do you want? This is Lord Lumley's land.'

'I know that, fellow,' Harman retorted, falling into the blustering manner that Revill knew all too well. 'And it's Lord Lumley himself I wish to see. A private matter between my master and His Lordship – which I don't intend to discuss with his servants.'

'I serve Sir Robert Cecil,' Gillan replied, his voice deepening almost to a growl. 'And it would be remiss of me to let you go further. So, unless you're willing to offer good reason for your visit, I'll request you turn your horse about and leave.'

There followed a brief silence. Revill glanced round, realising that the baggage cart had rolled on ahead of them. Further off, the hawking continued... but on the edge of the party, a figure on horseback had halted and was looking in their direction.

A RELUCTANT HERO

'See now, you've been spotted already,' Gillan said to Harman, jerking his thumb towards the watcher. 'Soon you'll have men-at-arms around you. Since you're a part of the Progress, you'll know folk are a mite jittery when it comes to the Queen's safety.'

'For God's sake, will you listen?' As usual, Harman was losing patience. 'I'm as loyal to the Queen as any man - and I'm here to carry a message, nothing more.' He drew a folded paper from his doublet, showed it and replaced it. 'If you must know, Lord Ballater writes to Lord Lumley to beg Her Majesty to change her mind, and grant him one more chance to present his petition. He wishes to come this evening, when she has returned from the chase.'

'Change her mind, you say?' Gillan wore a sceptical look. 'Why would she do that?'

For once, Harman hesitated – and Revill understood: the steward knew well enough that this was a fool's errand. Yet he was loyal to the last, and had gone along with his master's muddled hopes... for that at least, Revill almost respected him.

Gillan was about to speak again but stayed himself, for hoofbeats were approaching rapidly. Both he and Revill turned to see the man who had been observing them ride up. He drew rein swiftly, revealing himself as one of Lord Lumley's liveried attendants.

'What goes here, Daniel?' The man enquired. 'Another petitioner, is it?'

'In a manner, it is,' Gillan replied. 'This is Lord Ballater's steward, carrying a letter for your master. He appears to want to deliver it himself.'

'That I do,' Harman said stiffly, irked at being obliged to deal with men he considered beneath his station. 'It's a private matter, between peers of the realm.'

'Well then, I will convey it,' the attendant said, with a look that brooked no refusal.

Harman bristled. 'I'm grateful for the offer, but-'

'It's the only offer you will get, sir,' the other broke in. 'And you keep me from my duties. Hand the message to me, and you have my word that it will be passed to Lord Lumley.'

And there the matter rested. Stolidly, the three of them regarded Harman in silence, until at last he relented. With an impatient sigh he drew the paper out again, leaned from the saddle and handed it over. Lumley's man turned his horse, nodded briefly at Gillan and rode off. Harman would have ridden off too, had Revill not spoken up.

'How does His Lordship?' he enquired, with a bland look. 'Is he well?' And when Harman frowned: 'Or should I ask after Master Bridges? What happened three days back was a fearful shock to him, as I recall.'

'Damn you, Perrot!' With a glare, the steward raised his hand and pointed. 'I never trusted you, and now I trust you even less! Have you latched on to some other nobleman, like the burr that you are? Mayhap I'm not the only one who'd be glad to see the back of you!'

With that he tugged the rein harshly, making his horse jerk in alarm. Then he was urging the animal away, breaking into a gallop. Revill watched him go.

'Why did he call you Perrot?' Gillan enquired.

***

Two hours later, the mid-day stop for refreshment brought another surprise for Revill.

The day was hot, and the party had sought shade under a grove of trees. Servants had set out a table for the Queen and her closest companions, while others sat on the grass or walked about in casual conversation. Revill, sitting some distance away with Gillan, had lost sight of Sir Robert Cecil. Though he recognised other Privy Councillors, last seen when the Progress was approaching Chichester: Lord Chamberlain Hunsdon, for one. He was reminded of Cecil's words of the night before, about the need for other Crown Purveyors to take on the tasks left by Hooper and Godwin. But Hooper, presumably already despatched to London, was out of Revill's hands, and he was relieved not to concern himself with the man again - nor with Godwin, for that matter. Having turned attention to his empty stomach, he had eaten and drunk with relish when a figure approached on foot, to reveal himself as Lord Lumley's servant, who had taken the message from Harman.

'Captain Revill?' The man halted. 'My master asks you to attend him.'

'Indeed?' Revill blinked. 'Do you know why?'

'I do not. But if you'd care to follow me?'

'Well, I will.' Laying aside his costrel of ale, Revill got to his feet. As he did so, Gillan sniffed and looked up at him.

'First you're Perrot, now you're a Captain... I'm getting befuddled.'

Revill lifted a hand, before walking off. The gesture might have suggested that he would explain later; or perhaps it was merely to discourage questions.

A few minutes later he found himself standing under a huge beech tree, making his bow to Lord Lumley himself. To his further surprise there was no-one else within earshot, and the man who had brought him was ordered to step away. Whereupon the two faced each other, Revill waiting in silence for His Lordship to speak.

'I'm told – by Sir Robert Cecil, that is - that before arriving here at Stansted, you attended Lord Ballater,' were his first words.

'I did, my lord.'

'In what capacity did you serve?' The voice was soft, and so quiet Revill had to make an effort to hear.

'As a guard. He had – indeed he still has, few attendants.'

'And yet, you are not a man of his faith.'

'I'm not. Just an ex-soldier for hire, who'll put himself in harm's way if needed.'

Lord Lumley regarded him for a moment. 'Sir Robert has suggested that, to use your own words, you would put yourself in harm's way on anyone's account, if asked – even mine.'

'I would if you wished it, my Lord,' Revill said, in some surprise. 'But I don't understand... are you expecting trouble of some kind?'

Instead of answering the other looked away, in the direction of the Queen's party. Someone had produced a lute, and the strains of an old air drifted across the park.

'I heard you intercepted Lord Ballater's steward, bearing the message from his master,' he continued, without looking at Revill. 'As matters have turned out, the Queen will grant his request. Her party leaves here tomorrow for Portsmouth... hence, as a mark of favour, she has agreed to hear a number of petitions on this, her last evening at Stansted.'

Revill took in the news. He had the feeling he was about to be called upon to perform some task or other... until the man's next words caught him off guard.

'You weren't just a soldier, were you, Captain Revill?' His Lordship's gaze was upon him now, frank and clear-eyed. 'You were an intelligencer, charged with matters of intrigue... I might even say, of delicacy. Somewhat beyond the call of duty, for a fighting man.'

Having no ready reply, Revill remained silent.

'So - this is what I propose,' Lord Lumley continued. 'That when Lord Ballater arrives to pay homage to the Queen and present his petition, you will be close at hand, alert for any sign of... I almost said danger. But I think you understand well enough.'

With that, the man let out a sigh. 'There's no trust on the part of Privy Councillors, when it comes to men of my religion,' he added. 'Whatever we say or do, we're under suspicion. Sir Robert has formed a strong – one might say a rigid – notion that someone in Ballater's train poses a threat to the Queen. And you, it seems, having spent weeks in his company, know the men of his party better than anyone does. Hence, do you see how the land lies?'

'I do, my lord,' Revill answered... but his spirits sank. Once again, it seemed, he was about to be tasked with keeping watch on Ballater's men, though he had long ago dismissed Hawkins and Harman as unlikely assassins. And what of Shearer? he wondered. He was still a member of His Lordship's train... was he not as well placed as anyone, to be alert for any sign of trouble?

'I ask you to stand guard in the great hall, this night,' Lord Lumley said. 'To observe closely, and to be ready. Are you willing?'

'Your pardon, my Lord.' Revill met his eye. 'Does this order come from Sir Robert, or-'

A RELUCTANT HERO

'It does not,' the other broke in. 'Indeed, it's not an order at all. It's a private request from me, which you may decline. However, I do hope that you won't.'

And that, of course, was the reason Revill had been brought here. He was to be a guard, but an unofficial one, without warrant - or even the knowledge - of any of the important men who attended the Queen. An outsider who, in the unlikely event that a threat to Her Majesty arose, was supposed to intervene despite any risk to himself. Just then, the voice of his old gunnery corporal Tom Bright flew to his mind: *Sweet Jesus, Captain, what are you going to do now?*

Drawing a breath, Revill made his bow to Lord Lumley and assented.

***

The rest of the day passed without incident: a balmy, late August afternoon that fully merited the description of a *pique-nique* in the park. But for Revill, it had been something less: an afternoon of thinking too much about his new task, and all that might follow. When Gillan made conversation, he responded as he rode, yet his mind was elsewhere: chiefly on Ballater and his people, who would certainly accompany him on his visit to Stansted that evening. His hope was that he might get a chance to speak with Shearer before His Lordship's moment with the Queen arrived… or even with Hawkins, whom he had grown to trust. His feeling still was that there was no plot, and never had been: that the risks of such an action were too great, that Ballater was desperate for the Queen's mercy in offering a way to reduce his debts, and that neither of his followers – even the belligerent Harman - were murderers, let alone regicides.

Brooding on the matter as the sun waned, he followed the returning host and came at last to the Stansted stables. The yard was crowded and noisy, grooms hurrying to manage the nobles' horses while liveried servants, falconers and others moved about. One fact, at least, brought Revill a scrap of relief: the Queen had greatly enjoyed her day, and was said to be tired. Visitors and petitioners, the fortunate few who were to be granted an audience before the farewell feast in the great hall, would have only a very short time in her presence. His spirits lifting a little, he mentioned it to Gillan as they unsaddled their mounts.

'Farewell feast, you say?' The older man grunted. 'Not for the likes of us. Supper will be bread and a wedge of pie, and small beer instead of wine.'

To which, Revill hadn't the heart to tell him that he would not be sitting down with him in the Stansted kitchen, but was supposed to stand by while Lord Lumley's nobler guests assembled in the main hall. He wondered if Ballater would be among them, before dismissing the notion. The man was unwelcome and would probably arrive late, granted a moment merely because the Queen's host had asked on his behalf.

And on a sudden, after he had put Malachi to rest and was walking out into the evening sunshine, he stopped in his tracks. An image had arisen, of the bloated old lord waddling towards the royal chair, puffing and mouthing gruff compliments before being fobbed off with one of Queen Elizabeth's famous promises to consider the matter - which meant almost certain disappointment. Then, Revill had always believed Ballater's aspirations doomed, his insistence on following her summer progress a triumph of hope over reality.

'I think I'll take a walk,' he said, turning to Gillan. 'Been too long in the saddle.'

'Aren't you hungry?' The other enquired, stifling a yawn; it had been a long day, and he was weary. 'I'm for a swig of beer, and somewhere to rest my bones.'

'Later.' Throwing him a smile, Revill turned to walk out of the stable yard, away from the hubbub.

He had no particular need to walk, or even to think further about the evening ahead. Instead he was thinking of Jenna, and their cottage on Burwood's farm, and the promises he had made. Yet now, after all that had occurred, it looked as if the man who held Revill's future in his hands – Sir Robert Cecil – had almost abandoned him. He recalled Jenna's words, at their last meeting: could even Cecil be trusted to keep his word, in the matter of freeing him from the yoke he bore?

A RELUCTANT HERO

Leaving the stable yard behind, he strode out into the lane that skirted the paddock, increasing his pace. Thoughts rose – even a memory of Tom Bright and the portentous note he had left for Revill to find, back at the lodging in Dowgate. Could he still be in Portsmouth, or would he have taken ship by now? If so, would he ever see his old corporal again?

Walking steadily, though without purpose, he looked up from his reverie and found himself alone in the tree-lined lane, the avenue which led to the main gates of Stansted. Slowing to a halt, he decided he had best head back; at least he could take a mug with Gillan. He was about to do so when hooves sounded from behind. He turned sharply... and froze.

'Good God - of all people, see who stands in my way!' The rider cried, throwing out a gloved hand. 'But then, that's your occupation nowadays is it not, Revill? To thwart me, to forget all I've done for you - to hamper me at every turn! An ingrate, who cares not who he tramples on so long as he attains his desire. May God curse the ground you walk on!'

Upon which, breathing hard, Revill could do no more than stare up at his old spymaster, who glared down at him with a face of thunder.

Sir Thomas Heneage.

THIRTEEN

Heneage was not alone, but attended by a single servant, young and somewhat slight, mounted on a dappled gelding. He was leading another horse, laden with baggage. The two men had drawn rein before Revill, who stood immoveable in the middle of the lane.

'Sir Thomas,' he managed finally. 'Pray, don't tell me you're leaving?'

'By heaven, you'll not question me!' Heneage threw back in fury. 'I thought you'd sloped off by now, like the cur you are - instead, I hear you're hobnobbing with Privy Councillors, even Papists! Then, nothing was ever enough for you, was it? Despite the purses I allowed you, for such service as you gave – gave most grudgingly at that!'

'Yet despite those services, you tried to have me killed,' Revill said icily.

His anger had risen, smouldering and dangerous. Here at last was a chance to confront the man... and on a sudden, he felt reckless. He threw a glance at the servant, who looked nervous, and knew that he presented no threat.

'First, by a hired rogue,' he went on. 'And then by fire – except that your men fell somewhat short both times, did they not? Bryant, Hooper and Godwin and the others – all gone, and good riddance to them. And now you're almost alone, I see.' He jerked his head towards the young attendant. 'Your coffers running somewhat low, are they?'

To that, Heneage gasped; he was speechless with rage, but ultimately helpless. Revill saw it, as he observed the man's blotched complexion, the rheumy eyes: he looked as if he had barely slept in days. Whatever had passed between him and Sir Robert Cecil - if indeed, anything had passed - the fact remained that he was leaving the Queen's Progress: a clear mark of disfavour. Courtiers rose and fell, as they had always done: some by degrees, others swiftly. Heneage's enemies might have been tempted to gloat – but Revill felt only a burning resentment, at the hold this man had over him.

'A few weeks ago I was called to London, and went in good faith,' he said, as evenly as he could. 'I believed it was to be my last mission for you - and however unpleasant it might prove to be, I was prepared to see it through. I had no notion of what was to come – let alone that I would find myself stumbling upon a nest of rogues, who–'

'Stop that, damn you!'

Heneage had had enough. Clumsily, and to the alarm of his servant, he fumbled for his sword, drew it and raised it. At sight of which, Revill was almost inclined to laugh.

'Let's not be foolish,' he said. 'You know better than to challenge me.'

'Sir Thomas, please!' For the first time the young servant spoke up. 'You are yet on the Verge… this is madness.'

'Madness, is it?' Red-faced, Heneage turned on him. 'How dare you…'

But he faltered, panting. Spittle had appeared at his mouth, and after a moment he lowered the weapon. His actions had made his horse nervous. Revill took a pace forward and seized the bridle, making the animal flinch.

'I think you're unwell - sir,' he said. 'And it's a long ride back to London. Shouldn't you make haste while you can?'

A moment followed, one which would remain in Revill's memory for the rest of his days. It would be his last meeting with his one-time spymaster: a man in decline, whose powers were falling away. Letting go of the bridle, he stepped back and waited - whereupon Heneage played his last card, to devastating effect. After sheathing his sword, he raised a gloved hand and levelled it, somewhat shakily.

'You think you've triumphed, Revill,' he breathed. 'You think you're out of the woods – but you're wrong! I know what you've done, with your meddling – I don't forget, and I don't forgive. So I say this: think now, on your Papist sister and her husband - and remember that I'm still one of the Queen's Councillors, with the power to act! A request from me to the High Sheriff of Devonshire – a written accusation of Popish scheming – and they'll find themselves in Exeter gaol, awaiting trial. And I'll wager my last crown that the outcome of such a trial would be a forgone conclusion... do you see now? For I owe you, Revill, and I will pay you out. I will destroy you - and your family too!'

Standing rigid, Revill met his eye. On a sudden his worst fears, held in abeyance these past two years, seemed about to come to fruition. For a moment, he had an urge to seize Heneage and drag him from his horse, to throw all cares aside and slay the man on the spot...

But he did not. And though his heart sank, what remained was his innate strength: his soldier's stubbornness which, at the final turn, would sustain him. It would not be the first time he had been forced to act without hope, and likely it would not be the last. Drawing a long breath, he turned his eyes to the young attendant, who was clearly dismayed.

'I think you'd best set your master on his way now, don't you?' He suggested.

And without waiting for reply, he turned his back and began walking up the lane towards Stansted. He barely heard the hoofbeats, as they picked up again and faded into the distance.

***

That evening the hall of the great house, lavishly decorated with green boughs, flowers and hangings, was a splendid sight.

Even Revill, preoccupied as he was, saw that Lord Lumley had spared no pains to make the Queen's last night at his home an unforgettable one. Tables were set out, covered with Turkey carpets, laid with silverware and bowls of heaped fruit. In one corner, a consort of musicians was tuning lutes and viols as guests began to drift in. The conversation was loud, and tempered with relief: it was an open secret that many of the nobles were glad to be leaving the home of this Catholic lord, with all the tensions it had brought. Rumours of private ceremonies, held in remote parts of the house, had been rife for the last two days; as always, Revill had been alert to the kitchen gossip.

A RELUCTANT HERO

By now he had tidied his appearance as best he could, with the aid of a clean shirt loaned by Gillan. Along with servants wearing Lumley's livery, he made his way to the hall and took a position by one wall, beneath an array of hunting trophies. Not far away was a dais with an ornate chair for the Queen, where she would receive supplicants before the feast. Revill himself had no appetite: he had forgone supper, and the odour of roast meats and rich sauces wafting from the kitchens almost sickened him. His mind was filled with the encounter with Heneage: the sweaty face, scarlet with rage, sat starkly before him. How he was to act upon the man's threat he did not know; he had tried to tell himself that it was but a threat, and that the Vice-Chamberlain would have more than enough to occupy himself, instead of venting his rage on Revill's sister – merely for revenge, pure and simple.

And yet, he would not rest until he had got warning to Katherine. After the royal party had left Stansted, perhaps he could approach Sir Robert Cecil... whereupon he stiffened as, by coincidence, the man himself walked in.

If he caught sight of Revill, he gave no sign. Close behind him came Lord Lumley, dressed in a fine suit of dark silk, with his wife Lady Elizabeth at his side. At once the consort struck up, as the remaining members of Her Majesty's Progress began arriving in twos and threes. The hall was filling rapidly, servants hurrying about with stoups of wine. Guards with halberds marched in, and the air grew tense with expectation: the Queen was on her way. Revill's gaze swept the room as the company began to draw back, leaving a passage clear for the monarch. The guards lined up...and as if at a signal, a hush fell.

The music stopped, to be followed by the blast of a herald's trumpet, and Elizabeth entered, followed by her ladies-in-waiting. They made a splendid sight: a shining procession in silks and jewels, the Queen herself in a broidered silver gown spread over a huge farthingale. On her head was one of her numerous bright-red wigs, topped by a dressing of pearls, while her neck was hidden by a ruff of intricately-worked lace.

The effect, as intended, was almost magical: Astraea on earth, ageless and almost divine. Even Revill forgot all else, and bowed low with the entire company. It was the closest he had been to Elizabeth, and he had never seen her in all her finery. He was aware of a swish of heavy clothing, soft footsteps and even a tinkle of jewellery as the group passed. Then he stood upright, in time to see her mount the platform and sit. Courtiers gathered round, bringing seats for her ladies. There was some subdued talk on the dais, then movement from the other end of the hall, where a different gathering was taking place by the doorway. Looking round, Revill saw the first of the invited people, an elderly man, waiting to be summoned. Then a voice, loud and commanding.

'Her Royal Majesty will hear petitioners. Make way!'

And suddenly, he was doubly alert. There was no real cause, he told himself: it was clear that no-one who might pose a threat to the monarch would get a chance. Her favourites stood nearby: young gallants wearing swords, every one of them eager to win her attention. The older noblemen and Councillors, in gowns and gold chains, stood on their dignity – among them Sir Robert Cecil, dwarfed by those around him. And yet... again Revill's gaze scanned the crowded hall, coming to rest on the first petitioner, who was being led forward by a gentleman usher. Tearing off his hat, and somewhat overawed by the occasion, the old man made his way to the dais and knelt.

At which moment, with his eyes fixed on The Queen, Revill felt rather than saw someone move quietly up alongside him.

'That's William Marsh, farmer,' the newcomer whispered in his ear. 'Been trying to get his case heard for years, so I'm told. Mayhap it's hope that keeps him alive, eh?'

It was Shearer. Letting out a breath, Revill kept his gaze firmly on the monarch.

'Hope, you say?' He murmured. 'Perhaps that's what sustains most of us, nowadays.'

He glanced round to see his former companion wearing his best doublet, the sleeves newly slashed to show a yellow silk lining... whereupon, recalling his duties, he frowned.

'Is he here, then? Ballater?'

'He is,' came the reply. 'Waiting his turn like the rest. Harman's with him.'

A RELUCTANT HERO

'And Hawkins?'

'He's back there too. He was glad to get away for the evening.'

'Any particular reason?' Revill enquired, watching Master Marsh presenting his petition to the Queen. Elizabeth, however, kept her hands on her lap, allowing one of her attendants to take the paper. A few words of reassurance, a royal nod, and the old man's audience with his sovereign was over.

'Too many,' Shearer murmured in reply. 'Bridges' house is a place of misery... the poor man's too downcast to get out of his bed, and the servants are afraid to challenge Ballater. As a result, he rules the roost like a fat cockerel.'

'As he did from the start,' Revill said. 'And I wonder now if it was planned – I mean Harman taking over Bridges' house. A convenient base for His Lordship.'

The two of them fell silent, as another petitioner was being brought forward in place of Farmer Marsh. This was a woman, leading a small child. She approached the dais, curtseyed – and promptly burst into tears. Clearly, the occasion was too much.

'How many more are waiting?' Revill asked, under his breath. But for answer, Shearer merely touched his arm. Looking round, he saw the next petitioner – an elegant man, probably a merchant of some kind – standing ready.

And just behind him, stood Lord Ballater.

Fully alert, Revill fixed his gaze on the familiar figure, gaudily dressed and leaning heavily on his cane. If anything, the man's enormous bulk seemed to have increased in the days since he had left his service. The face was puffed, the large feathered hat askew... in fact, His Lordship appeared ill-at-ease. Then, seeing that after months of waiting he was at last being allowed to approach the Queen, nervousness was understandable. At his side was Harman, standing rigid.

'What did I say about hopes?' Shearer murmured. 'It'll all be over in a trice, and to no avail. The Queen would no more grant him a favour than kiss him.'

'And Harman knows it,' Revill said. 'He's always known it.'

It was true: the blustering steward, who had made life difficult for him from the start, now cut a forlorn figure. The entire project

– the weeks of trailing after the Queen, of keeping apart under constant suspicion because of his faith - had finally told on the man to the extent that, to Revill's eyes at least, he looked beaten. What future was there for him now, as head of a shrinking household under an impoverished and deluded master like Ballater? A dreary return to His Lordship's estate, with the prospect of land being sold off piecemeal to pay debts and recusancy fines, was all that lay ahead.

Not for the first time, Revill came close to pitying him.

But there came a stir from the dais, prompting him to turn. The lady petitioner, subdued and with her child clutching at her skirts, was being led away. The Queen, meanwhile, sat stately and unmoved, the picture of royal dignity; if she was finding the procession of plaintiffs tiresome, she showed no sign. Soon the well-dressed merchant was being ushered forward, to make his bow and drop to one knee before Elizabeth.

More confident than the previous petitioners, the man held out his paper firmly, murmuring some prepared words. He even made a bold attempt at humour: one or two of the Queen's ladies could be heard to chuckle, while Gloriana herself summoned a smile. Polite words were exchanged, to be followed by another royal nod; perhaps this request would receive slightly more consideration than the others, Revill thought. As the merchant rose to take his leave, he scanned those nearest to the Queen, satisfied that a careful watch was being kept, no matter how unlikely the threat. He even allowed his mind to stray to his own troubles, until a nudge from Shearer made him stiffen: Lord Ballater was about to have his turn.

Removing his hat, His Lordship handed it to Harman and took his first, unsteady steps forward, aided by his cane. Clearly his strength had waned, as he carried his enormous frame through the crowd of watchers, few of whom would have known who he was. The usher, after a few words with Ballater and Harman, allowed the steward to assist his master. And so at last the two of them, arm in arm, came into the monarch's presence and bowed.

Taut as a post, Revill pressed forward. As he did so he caught sight of Sir Robert Cecil, who had stepped from the throng of courtiers to stand closer to the Queen. And at once, the air was filled with portent: the moment had come, when the suspicions Cecil held would be justified, or proved baseless. And yet, after all that had happened, only one of the men Revill had been told to watch remained: Harman, looking strained with concern for His Lordship. No matter how deep his Catholic faith, no matter now powerful his resentment at the plight of men like his master, the man was no murderer, let alone a slayer of Queens. Revill had long ago formed that view, and was as certain of it now as he had ever been. When all was said and sifted, his mission had been a wild goose chase.

And so like everyone else, he stood and watched as Ballater, stifling a cough, spoke low to Elizabeth. The words were difficult to hear from where he stood, but he believed His Lordship's address began with an apology for his inability to kneel, on pain of not being able to rise again. This was followed by what sounded like a plea to Her Majesty, mercifully without it descending into a list of grievances. Then came a surprise: a gift of a tiny, jewelled box for Elizabeth, which Ballater held forth; it had been his late wife's, he said, and he begged her to accept it.

A low murmur rippled through the watchers – mostly of approval, though there were a few frowns from the courtiers. The Queen, however, rose to the occasion with her customary aplomb, taking the box from His Lordship's hand before passing it to one of the women-in-waiting. An expression of thanks followed, then a few words conveying the usual promise to consider the petitioner's case. Taking the cue, Harman rose from his knees, bowed and took his master's arm, ready to help him away.

It was over, and the danger was past. Revill let out a sigh, feeling his whole body loosen as the tension lifted...

Until the unthinkable happened.

Throwing Harman aside with a sudden and alarming display of strength, Lord Ballater raised his cane, gripped the handle and, with a movement that brought a gasp from a hundred throats, drew a thin blade from within it, as long as his forearm. At the same time, his mouth opened and a shout came forth, that stunned the entire company.

'Glory to the true God, and death to Elizabeth! Heretic and bastard daughter of the Devil's whore, Anne Boleyn! See how she dies!'

And as those about stood rooted in horror – even the gallants, of whom the quickest were only now reacting – a stark reality dawned: that they had been caught utterly off guard, and it was too late. In plain sight the threat was laid bare – no chimera, but a cold and terrible truth: the Queen was about to die, by the most violent means.

Or so she would have been, had not Ballater broken into a sudden, hacking cough. For a second he wavered, before mastering himself and preparing to lurch forward...

By which time, Revill had acted.

There was no time to think, only to move as would a soldier in combat: to react at speed without fear of consequence. Springing forward, he covered the distance to the Queen's dais and seized Ballater's arm – stopping the blade he was about to thrust, barely a foot from her chest. Frozen in the moment, he saw her elaborately embroidered stomacher, the glint of sapphires and rubies... he even caught the scent of perfume. Then he grew aware of shouts, of the screams of women, and of bodies crowding in from all sides. Yet he held on to Ballater's arm in its thickly padded sleeve, using all his strength to force it aside, dogged persistence his spur: he would thwart the man's intent, or die trying. Meanwhile his opponent wheezed and cursed, his sour breath in Revill's face...

But he was weakening. No match for Revill, he sagged - and at last a mass of men fell upon him, throwing him to the ground and piling on top of him. Revill was shoved aside roughly, his hand torn from its grasp on Ballater's arm as another hand emerged to seize the slender blade. There was a yelp as blood was drawn... whereupon from somewhere far away, came a sound that shook him almost as much as the tussle.

It was Harman, crying out desperately: 'Lord God, forgive him... in thy name, have pity!'

Then a flailing fist came up from somewhere in the melee, and knocked Revill out cold.

A RELUCTANT HERO

FOURTEEN

When he returned to consciousness a few minutes later, his first thought that he was on some battlefield. There was commotion all about, a flurry of movement and a buzz of voices. Then another voice, very close, addressing him.

'Can you see? You took a knock, but nothing more... you'll be right as rain.'

Blinking, he shifted his gaze to see Shearer crouching beside him. He was lying on the floor of the great hall, close to the wall where he had stood earlier, his head resting on something soft. It took him a moment to realise that the pillow was Shearer's doublet with its silk lining, and its owner was in shirt sleeves.

'Is she safe?' He muttered. 'I mean the-'

'The Queen is quite safe,' Shearer broke in. 'They took her off to her chamber to rest. The feast is cancelled - a sore blow to Lumley. The man's grief-stricken... blames himself.'

'By the Christ.' Revill lifted a hand and felt his head, which was throbbing. There was a lump, but no blood.

'What of Ballater?' He asked. 'Did they kill him?'

'They didn't need to,' Shearer answered, with some distaste. 'He spared them the trouble, as he's spared himself the ordeal of trial and execution. The whole, wild scheme was too much for him. By the time they'd disarmed him he was dying... heart gave out, I suspect. At the final turn, he lost.'

For Revill, the reality sank in slowly. A vivid picture of Ballater, his face filled with anguish as he wrestled for the blade he had concealed, rose starkly. And with a further shock, he recalled now that he had heard words, hissed between clenched teeth as the man saw that he had failed: that the desperate attempt of one who was already dying, had failed utterly.

'My son,' Ballater had gasped. 'I give my life for you, and for God!'

Revill let out a long breath, and sat up slowly. 'So, I was mistaken – as Cecil was mistaken. There was no killer in Ballater's train: not Dickon of course, nor Hawkins, nor Harman. The assassin was Ballater himself.'

'And yet, in a way Cecil was right,' Shearer said. 'There was a plot hatched within his household, even if the perpetrator was the one I least suspected.'

'As did I,' Revill admitted.

Looking about, he saw that the hall was empty of guests, leaving only servants to clear the tables. Lord Ballater's body had been removed, and the Queen's dais was empty. With an effort he got to his feet, waving aside Shearer's offer of a hand to aid him.

'I could use a drink,' he said finally.

'I rejoice to hear it,' was the reply.

But as they began to move, Revill stopped with a frown. 'What have they done with Harman?'

Shearer merely shook his head, and turned towards the doorway.

***

Some hours later, taking a cup of strong sack in the kitchen, Revill was surprised to be ordered to attend Sir Robert Cecil.

It was Daniel Gillan who brought the order. Looking Revill up and down, as he sat in a corner with Shearer, he halted and shook his grey head.

'By God, you've a nose for trouble, have you not?' He muttered. 'Only now you're a hero, I heard. Put yourself between the Queen and a madman with a stick, is what they're saying. I don't know whether to fall at your feet, or steer clear of you.'

'Why not take a mug with me instead?' Revill said. 'Now I think on it, I should have done that after we got back from the hawking.'

'I would, gladly,' Gillan answered. 'But this isn't the time.' He relayed the instruction: that Revill was to accompany him at once to the cerise chamber, where Cecil waited.

'Well, that's interesting,' Shearer remarked. 'Will there be a reward, I wonder? Or, knowing our diminutive master as I do, is it more likely that you're about to be berated for allowing the situation to arise? The man has a knack for shifting blame.'

A RELUCTANT HERO

'I'll pretend I didn't hear that - sir,' Gillan said, with a frosty look. 'Sir Robert's a true servant of the Queen, who'd put her life before his at any time. He deserves respect.'

'A jest, my friend, nothing more.' Shearer threw him a wry smile, and lifted his mug. Turning to Revill, he said: 'Good luck… I drink to you in the hope you won't need it.'

Gillan had already stepped away, so Revill rose to follow him out of the kitchen: now a subdued place, rife with mutterings. Untouched food was everywhere, along with stacks of borrowed pewter. As he left, there were glances aimed in his direction.

In the passage outside, Gillan turned to him. 'So, how should I address you now? Perrot, or Revill - or Captain?'

'You can call me Will,' came the reply. 'I'm no longer a captain. Shall we proceed?'

The cerise chamber turned out to be a small room on an upper floor of the house. Here Sir Robert Cecil sat behind a carved table with quills and writing materials. When Revill and Gillan entered, he bade them close the door and waved them forward. Gillan stood back, however, leaving Revill to approach the table.

'I'm supposed to be elsewhere, just now,' Cecil said, without preamble. 'Downstairs the Privy Council is meeting in private session. Hence, I'll be brief.'

Standing stolidly, Revill waited.

'Her Majesty the Queen wishes me to convey her thanks for your bold intervention,' the man continued, in a dry tone. 'Though, had her attendants not acted as promptly as they did, you might not be here to receive them. You were precipitate and clumsy, Revill. And once again you appear to have forgotten - or even ignored – my orders. You're undisciplined… a danger, I might add, even to yourself.'

He paused, and fixed Revill with a gaze that shook him. Shearer's remark from but a few minutes ago came to his mind: *More likely you're about to be berated…* Biting back a reply, he kept his silence. Had he not, he wondered, saved the Queen's life? Or were those terrible events in the great hall about to be moulded to fit some other narrative of the Council's choosing? *A madman with a stick*, Gillan had said – was that how the incident was to be reported?

'And yet, it's fitting that you should have some reward,' Cecil was saying. 'Call it a final payment, for the services you rendered.'

He turned aside, opened a wooden casket and drew out a small purse... and in an instant, Revill's mind flew back to those times with Heneage, when he had been paid in similar fashion. Yet here was the new spymaster: as ruthless a man as his predecessor, but more controlled and far cleverer. Would Cecil throw the purse to him as Heneage was wont to do, he wondered, forcing him to catch it?

He did not. Instead, he pushed it to the edge of the table and sat back. The silence grew, until Revill could stand it no longer.

'I acted as best I could, Sir Robert,' he said tightly. 'And if I failed to discover Lord Ballater's true intent, I was hardly alone in that. And more...'

He stopped himself: his anger was rising, and must be curbed. He was no longer an agent of Cecil's, charged with uncovering a conspiracy: Ballater was dead, his household in disarray. The mission was ended, and Revill just another ex-soldier again. On a sudden he thought of Hawkins, and wondered whether he had fled, or was taken captive...

'And more?' Cecil turned a cold eye upon him. 'Pray, do continue. If you have something to say before we part, I will hear it.'

Revill hesitated, then framed his question. 'Might I ask what's been done with Ballater's people? His steward, Harman... it's my belief that the man was unaware his master was planning to act as he did. The same's true of his other servant, Hawkins.'

'That's your belief, is it?' Cecil enquired. And when Revill made no answer: 'Would it surprise you to learn that Ballater's steward has already been put to hard question, and admitted his guilt?'

'It does surprise me,' Revill admitted, with a frown.

'Well, it shouldn't,' the other snapped. 'You, of all people, know the truth regarding the Papists. I don't believe a single one of them who would have tried to stop Lord Ballater, had they known what he intended.'

A RELUCTANT HERO

'And yet, sir....' Drawing a breath, Revill eyed him. 'Whatever Harman admitted under hard question, I maintain my opinion that Hawkins is innocent of any involvement. He may be a Papist, but he fought for the Crown in Ireland... he's as loyal as I am.'

'Indeed?' For the first time, a slight smile played over the little Councillor's features. 'Well then, it's his grave misfortune to have served a man like Ballater. Misfortune, or poor judgement. But in any case...' he shrugged. 'They'll both hang. Any threat to the Queen's person, real or perceived, is treason. My advice to you is to dismiss all memory of them, and be on your way.'

And with that, the meeting was over. Sitting back again, Cecil merely assumed a stony gaze and waited. For his part, though with a heavy heart, Revill could no nothing other than reach forward and pick the purse up from the table, feeling its lightness as he did so. This was his reward: to take the meagre fee, make himself scarce and forget all that had happened.

We're deniable, Shearer had said. He might have added that men like them were mere implements, Revill thought - to serve their purpose, and then be discarded.

Forcing himself to make a bow, he turned in silence and headed for the door. As he passed Gillan, the older man threw him a glance of what looked like sympathy. Then he was outside, walking to the stairhead, increasing his pace as he descended. He was bound for the stables, to look in on Malachi.

Just now, he had no desire for human company,

***

The following day Revill was up before dawn, leaving the servants in the cramped chamber asleep. A restlessness consumed him: a need to be on the road out of Stansted – indeed, to be out of Hampshire without delay. He would ride to Devon – almost two hundred miles, he estimated, before he could reach Katherine and her husband to warn them. Somehow, they must then forge a plan of escape: he could not afford to take the chance that Sir Thomas Heneage's words held only an empty threat. When that was done he would ride back to Burwood's farm and take Jenna away, though he knew not where.

The previous night, he had bidden farewell to Gillan. There was warmth between them, along with regret at what had occurred, but the man was calm: he would pass his last days in Cecil's service, then fade into a quiet old age. The grisly - and unlawful - business following events at the Purveyors' hut had subdued him, perhaps more than Revill had realised. After taking the promised mug together in the kitchens, they had shaken hands and gone to their beds; Revill would be away before the other was even awake.

Which left only Shearer - who for some reason had disappeared after Revill had left him in the kitchen to attend Cecil. And yet, though he owed the man his life and wished to thank him again, there was no time. With dawn beginning to break, he entered the deserted stables and took Malachi from his stall. After saddling him he led him out to the yard, grimly aware that he had no food or drink to sustain him on the journey ahead; nor even a pack, since he had lost almost everything in the fire at Bridges' house. But he had the purse from Cecil, which would see him through. He was preparing to mount when a whistle from somewhere startled him... one that was familiar, following that fateful night at the Purveyors' hut.

'I had a notion you'd be leaving as soon as day broke,' Shearer said, walking up swiftly. 'Another minute and you'd have been gone... which would have been be a pity.'

'I'm glad you've waylaid me,' Revill said, turning to face him. 'And in the nick of time, once again. How shall I fare now, without you to watch my back?'

'Well, as it happens, I didn't come to bid you goodbye just yet,' the other said. 'And if you'll allow me, I'll explain.'

Surprised, Revill signalled his assent.

'In truth, I've been a bit of a rogue,' Shearer went on. 'Broken the law, and taken what might be the biggest risk of my life. But then...' He paused, shaking his head. 'I couldn't see the man hang - I just couldn't.'

'What man?' Revill demanded sharply. 'You don't mean Harman?'

'Of course not,' Shearer said, with a touch of scorn. 'I mean Hawkins. He may be a clod, but he's an honourable clod – and he doesn't deserve the gibbet. So, to cut the tale short, I've sprung him from prison. Or rather, I unlocked the cellar door before anyone was about, and got him out of the house. He's hiding now, somewhere down the lane.'

'He's *what*?' Revill's jaw dropped. 'Sweet Jesus, you-'

'I know!' Shearer broke in. 'But we don't have time to debate the rightness of my actions. If you'll saddle his horse and take it to him as you leave here, he'll be ready. He can be well clear of Stansted before he's found missing.'

'But what of Harman?' Revill demanded, his mind racing. 'You left him-'

'To hang – indeed I did. From what I know now, he's guilty as sin. It was he who arranged to have Hawkins lured away, the night of the fire…' Breaking off, Shearer shook his head. 'But forget him, will you? Just set our old drinking-companion safely on his way. I know you can do it – as I know you want to see him a free man. There's no time to lose – the Progress leaves today, and the Queen's servants are already rising.'

'And what of you?' Revill demanded. 'If you've truly taken the biggest risk of your life, which seems likely. Are you certain no-one saw you set Hawkins free? What if Harman spills the tale?'

'Somehow, I don't think he will,' Shearer said. 'But in that, I'll have to trust to luck.'

'So, you're staying here?'

'I'm Cecil's man, am I not?' For the first time, Shearer showed weariness. 'He expects me to remain with the Progress. The Queen will need guarding even more closely, when she arrives at Southampton. But later on…' He gave a shrug. 'Who knows, I might even turn up on your doorstep one day, and drag you off to get drunk.'

'I thought you were part of the garrison at Portsmouth,' Revill began… but at the look on the other's face, he frowned.

'Did you?' Shearer smiled.

And with that he stuck out his hand, needing no further words. Revill grasped it, then drew him close. The embrace was brief before they parted, Shearer disappearing as swiftly as he had arrived. For his part, leaving Malachi's rein to trail, Revill hurried back into the stable to locate Hawkins's horse, which he identified in the gloom with some difficulty. Working fast, he took the nearest saddle and bridle, readied the animal and then led it outside… to stop abruptly. Two grooms, young men in shirt sleeves and fustian, were crossing the yard in his direction.

'Good morning,' Revill said, summoning a cheerful smile. 'Up and eager, eh?'

To his relief, the youths smiled in return.

'Indeed, sir,' one said. 'The Queen's men are out already… Stansted will be as good as empty by mid-day.'

'Then I must make haste to join the exodus,' Revill replied. Leading Hawkins' mount forward, he caught up Malachi's rein. 'And I thank you for looking after this fellow,' he added. 'It's been… a most interesting stay, for all of us.'

With that he turned away, drawing both horses behind him; he barely noticed the stable-lads touching their caps in deference. Had they known that he was about to help a presumed felon escape execution, he would think later, they might have acted differently.

But already the sun was rising, on what promised to be another warm day. Walking faster, aware of noises ahead, he led the horses past the paddock and out towards the lane… where he halted. The area before the great house was now a scene of activity, with half-laden carts, grunting oxen and servants scurrying about. Men-at-arms in royal livery were gathered by the doorway in subdued conversation; doubtless the attempt on the Queen's life the evening before would be the over-riding topic. Wary of being recognised, Revill was anxious to get clear; already he had attracted more attention than he liked. He was drawing the animals forward again, when a shout startled him. Slowly he looked round, to see someone striding purposefully towards him… and when recognition dawned, he stiffened.

'Here you are, Captain Revill,' the man said. 'I was afraid you were gone from us already.'

Revill made no answer, standing with reins in both hands. Before him was Lord Lumley's attendant, the one who had interrupted the confrontation between him and Harman in the park.

A RELUCTANT HERO

Was it only the day before? Somehow, it seemed an age ago... drawing a breath, he faced him and nodded a greeting.

'In truth, I should be on my way,' he said, thinking fast. 'My work is over, and I have company to keep. Hence, I must bid you good morning.'

'Could you not spare a moment first?' The man enquired. 'For my task now is as it was yesterday, at the hawking. In short, my master has charged me with finding you and bringing you to him forthwith. I believe he wants to thank you, for what you did yesternight.'

'I'm humbled,' Revill managed to say. 'Yet I've already been rewarded, and desire no further thanks. Some... family business awaits me.'

'It would take only a short while,' the other persisted. 'Lord Lumley seldom makes such a request, of any man. I believe it would be to your benefit.'

He spoke courteously, but there was stubbornness in his manner. At once Revill was on his guard, thoughts flying up: Hawkins' escape was discovered... Shearer had been arrested...

'Then I must beg His Lordship's pardon,' he said. 'But as I said, I'm in haste-'

'Captain Revill, please.' The attendant used the same tone as when they had last set eyes on each other: one that would brook no refusal. He even placed a hand on his sword-hilt for good measure. Taut as a post, Revill glanced over his shoulder, and saw that resistance was too great a risk. Before he could even get mounted, a shout and a drawn sword would bring men running.

Letting out a sigh, he gave a nod and turned to lead the horses back to the stable. Briefly he thought of Hawkins, hiding somewhere down the lane and in fear for his life.

But the meeting with Lord Lumley, when it followed, would prove to hold no danger at all to Revill: quite the opposite, in fact.

***

To his surprise they did not enter the great house. Instead, the stern-faced attendant led him around the west wing to a pleasant knot-garden at the rear, laid out with beds of flowers and sweet-smelling herbs. Stone seats were set at intervals, and on the far side gardeners were already at work. It was far too early, of course, for members of the royal party to be taking a stroll in the sunshine before their departure. Indeed, Revill had begun to wonder why Lord Lumley would be up a such an hour - if indeed he was up, and this was merely a pretext. His breath tight, poised to react at the first sign of deception, he walked onto the neatly-trimmed grass... and blinked.

Just ahead of him, Lumley himself rose from a seat and came forward. He was wearing a broidered morning gown, and low-heeled leather slippers. And as with their last meeting, under a tree in the park, his attendant was waved away to leave the two of them alone. With pulse racing, Revill halted and made his bow. But when he stood up again, he was dumbfounded: the man looked exhausted.

'I spoke with Sir Robert Cecil, late last night,' Lord Lumley said in the soft, doleful tone Revill remembered. 'He was, shall I say, less than willing to speak at any length about you - the man who saved Her Majesty from almost certain death. I found that hard to compass... and hard to bear.'

Embarrassed, Revill lowered his gaze.

'And yet I insisted,' His Lordship resumed. 'I wished to know more of you, after what you did. In the end I learned enough... in particular, I learned of your relations with Sir Thomas Heneage, who has now departed. I'll not sadden you by recounting what you already know.'

As the words sank in, Revill was stunned. He had expected the worst: now it seemed that Lumley's attendant had spoken the truth. He was here to be thanked... but almost at once, his relief was tempered with urgency. He should have been gone by now, getting Hawkins horsed and riding away at speed; soon Cecil too would be up, and likely displeased to find him still here. Searching for words, he realised that Lord Lumley was speaking again, lowering his voice though there was no-one in earshot.

'You have a sister, in difficulties,' he murmured. 'Because of her faith... the same faith as mine, I might add. Though of course, you already know that.'

With a start, Revill looked up.

A RELUCTANT HERO

'Hence, a notion came to my mind… during the night, it was,' His Lordship continued. 'I discussed it with my wife, and she has concurred with me. It's the best solution, I believe. One that satisfies justice and benefits us all - aside from your master Sir Robert, I suspect. Hence, it must remain secret between us. Will you swear to that, before I say more?'

'My Lord, I will.' Amazed, Revill met his eye. 'And if I might lay to rest one other matter, Sir Robert is no longer my master. Whatever passes between us will go no further.'

'That's well,' came the reply. 'Besides, you'll soon have a lot to do, I imagine…' Lumley paused, his gaze straying across the rose-beds to where his gardeners were making strenuous efforts to look busy. Then he turned back to Revill, and spoke the words that would change his life. More importantly, they would do more than change the lives of his sister Katherine and her husband: they would save them. And thereafter he listened intently, and felt a sensation he hadn't felt in a long while.

It was something akin to joy.

FIFTEEN

Unbeknown to Revill – and unbeknown to most people, it seemed - Lord Lumley owned land in Ireland. He had only been there once, he said, a long time ago, and did not expect to go again. There was too much to occupy him here... and besides, under a cloud as he now was, it was impossible for him to leave England. On his land, he told Revill, were several small farms held by tenants under a steward. One of the farmers was now widowed, enfeebled and struggling. The obvious solution was that a younger man and wife should take up residence to manage the place. Only people of the Catholic faith would be welcome there, Lumley said; and so, it was all for the best.

In growing astonishment, Revill had taken up His Lordship's offer of a place on the stone bench, where they sat together.

'The farm is in Meath, on the Blackwater River,' Lumley was saying. 'A green and fertile place... and quite beautiful. Crops grow and beasts thrive, though there are said to be wolves in the hills. Do you think your sister and her husband would thrive there too?'

'They would, my lord,' Revill answered quietly. 'Indeed, merely to be able to practice their faith without fear of censure, or even arrest, would give them the strength to run a dozen farms. It's been a torment to them, to lose the one they had.'

'Well then, hear this,' His Lordship replied. 'I've a confession to make: I've already written a letter to my steward, which you may take to your sister and her spouse, who should then present it to him. I've drawn a map and directions for them, once they arrive in Dublin.'

With a sigh, Revill turned to face him. 'When I was brought here, I was told that you wished to thank me,' he said. 'Now I see that it's I who must proffer thanks... which would be inadequate. I will never be able to repay such kindness, as long as I live.'

A RELUCTANT HERO

To that, however, Lord Lumley made no reply, his face grave. Finally he met Revill's gaze, and shook his head.

'Can you imagine what would have happened,' he asked, 'had Lord Ballater succeeded in carrying out his desperate act yesterday? Can you think what the consequences would be – not just for myself, my wife and my entire household, but for every other person of our religion in this county, if not in all England?' He paused. 'And yet, as a soldier who as fought for the Queen, perhaps you can imagine it. I will say nothing further.'

'Nor need you, my lord,' Revill said. 'I can only give thanks that a catastrophe was averted. Those moments will stay with me, I'm certain, for the rest of my days.'

'And what will you do, with the rest of your days?' The other enquired, raising his eyebrows. 'An ex-soldier's life is precarious. Yet, I suspect you have no wish to accompany your sister to Ireland and turn farmer. Somehow, I cannot see you behind a plough.'

'Perhaps not,' Revill said, with a wry smile. 'I plan to marry, as soon as I can. After that, we'll forge a future somewhere… just now, it doesn't trouble me too much where that is.'

'Then, I can only wish you good fortune,' Lord Lumley said. He stood up, and reached inside the deep pocket of his morning-gown. A roll of papers appeared, bound with silk cord and tagged with his seal. A purse followed, which he held out on the palm of his hand.

'Enough to help your people take ship to Ireland, Captain Revill.'

Revill rose, drew a breath and took the purse. He made his bow, then straightened up and murmured his thanks, which fell far short of expressing what he felt. He was taking a step back when His Lordship stayed him.

'I should have said that, had you a notion to cross the Irish Sea with your relatives, there's enough there to pay for it,' he said. 'The farm will likely be run-down by the time they arrive, and will demand a great deal of work. Do you have anyone else in mind, who might help them make a start?'

In answer, Revill was about to shake his head until it struck him - so forcibly that he almost blurted it out, before seizing control of himself.

'As it happens, my Lord, I believe I do,' he said.

To which Lumley nodded, and bade him farewell. Never, he thought as he walked away, had a member of the nobility treated him with such grace and courtesy, let alone done so much with a purse and a letter – and words that had lifted his burden from his shoulders, in a matter of minutes.

***

The lane from Stansted was as yet deserted, the Royal Progress not expected to leave for some hours. Revill rode Malachi at a modest pace, leading Hawkins' horse behind, alert for a sign of the fugitive. But there was no movement from the trees and bushes that lined the avenue, nor any sound save that of birdsong. He was almost at the entrance when, at last, there came a voice from beside one of the gateposts. Reining in sharply, he called out - to be greeted by a bedraggled figure lurching into sight. Startled, he peered down at the ex-soldier, last seen face-to-face in the inn at Chichester, and let out a breath.

'Are you hurt?' he enquired, as Hawkins drew near.

'Only my feet, by God,' came the gruff reply. 'I left that cellar so quick, I hadn't time to put my shoes on. Ran for my life.' He paused, gazing up. 'But in God's name, I'm glad to see you. Shearer said you wouldn't forsake me... I wasn't sure I could believe him, until now.'

'You'd best get mounted,' Revill said, throwing a swift glance up the lane. 'I have some money. But once we've put a few miles between us and Stansted, I've a proposition for you. It might even be the answer to your prayers.'

'Eh?' Hawkins looked baffled. But when Revill gestured impatiently, he took the reins off him and stepped away. His relief at being reunited with his horse was so great, he was close to tears. After stroking the animal's neck, he put foot in stirrup and hauled himself tiredly into the saddle. Here was another, Revill thought, who had spent a sleepless night.

A RELUCTANT HERO

For a quarter-hour the two of them rode in silence, heading west. His companion, his face set in a grimace, seemed barely to notice the direction until Revill drew Malachi to a halt.

'Is this where we part?' Hawkins asked, reining in. 'If so, you have my thanks for-'

'Not just yet,' Revill said. 'I've money for you, and you'd better take my costrel to quench your thirst. It's a long journey to where you're going... or at least, where I hope you're going.' He nodded towards some trees, set back from the road. 'Shall we talk over there?'

'Do we need to?' Hawkins frowned.

Without answering, Revill turned Malachi and walked him off the road, up a bank and into the trees. Here he waited until his companion joined him, to sit in the saddle with a look of suspicion. But quite soon, as the proposal unfolded, his expression changed: to disbelief - and finally to astonishment.

It did not take long to explain. After relating his conversation with Lord Lumley, and speaking of his sister and her husband, Revill laid the plan out. If Hawkins would ride to Devon, to a place where he would direct him, and hand over the papers, he could then offer his services to Katherine, on her brother's recommendation. He would act as guard to her and her husband on the journey to Ireland, then help them take over the farm. In time, perhaps Hawkins might wish to move on... but he would at least be safe, to decide his next course. Revill had not forgotten their conversation, in Chichester. Now, as fate would have it...

'I'm offering you a chance,' he said, eyeing Hawkins frankly. 'The chance of a new life, or at least an escape from your old one. You might want to change your name...' he smiled briefly. 'You knew me as Perrot, but I'm Will Revill. I was a gunnery captain, who fought for the French king. So...' he gave a shrug. 'There you have it.'

For a while, Hawkins was speechless. He seemed to have difficulty grasping the import of what he had heard; it even appeared, at one point, as if he disliked the proposition. But at last, to Revill's relief, he let out a breath and sagged in the saddle. When he spoke, however, it was of a different matter entirely.

'I wouldn't want you to think ill of me... Captain Revill,' he said, in a subdued tone. 'So let me swear to you now, that I had no inkling of what Lord Ballater intended to do. Nor does that amaze me now, for he never trusted me enough to confide such a plan. He knew I would try to stop him. A man of his own faith I may be, but I'm no murderer.'

'I know that,' Revill said. 'As Shearer knows it, or he would not have aided you as he did.'

'That's true,' Hawkins breathed. 'And what does amaze me is, after I first set eyes on you in Mistress Bradby's house by Farnham, that I would end up owing my life to you, as well as to him...' he shook his head. 'And I was all set to fight you both, that night in Chichester.'

'It wouldn't have worked,' Revill said. 'Given your state, you'd have fallen over.'

'I would!' Hawkins agreed, growing animated on a sudden. The reality of his imminent salvation, it seemed, was dawning on him at last. 'Mercy, what a farrago it's been since then...' he stopped, a frown coming on.

'Harman knew,' he said, lowering his gaze.

Revill frowned too.

'He knew what was afoot,' Hawkins went on, 'and he believed you were a threat. He wanted you scratched from the page, just as His Lordship did. So when a message came, warning Harman that something was going to happen that night at the outhouse, he knew he had to get me clear. Though he didn't know a fire was to be set, he swears. He paid Bridges' cook, that sly fellow who panders his wenches under Bridges' nose. Margaret was one of them – she was told to lure me away for the night, and so leave the way open for you to perish. He looked up. 'Shearer's death too, would have made it look like an accident... an act of God, they'd have called it.'

'Likely they would,' Revill said, sobered by his testimony. But in his mind the last piece of the puzzle fell into place: Heneage, of course, was the one who had arranged to have the message sent. The mystery was explained – as was Godwin's ignorance of the ill-conceived fire, which he had doubted. He remembered the cook making a great show of trying to help, as had Harman - and yet he felt no anger now, even towards Ballater's steward. He recalled his last sight of the man - and his anguished words: *Lord God, forgive him...*

'So, he knew of Ballater's intent, and did nothing to stay him?' he asked finally.

'His Lordship was dying,' Hawkins said. 'He must have seen it as his last act – a blow for his religion. He'd lost everything... knew he wouldn't see his son again. Harman's devoted to His Lordship, so he humoured him - but he never truly believed he would carry out the deed. He didn't even know there was a blade hidden in the cane... Ballater got it from somewhere, I know not where.' He shook his head, then added: 'One good thing, at least, may follow: poor Master Bridges will be free of us all, to pick up his life again. It was a sad day for him when we came, and ended up making him a prisoner in his own house.'

He let out a sigh. 'I know this because Harman told me last night – told me everything. His last confession, since there'll be no priest to hear it where he's going. He's ready to die. Though what manner of death it will be, I don't dare to think on...'

With a sad look he trailed off, and Revill understood. Hawkins hated to leave Harman to his fate, and would regret it for the rest of his days. But he turned away, glancing towards the road: they had delayed long enough. Reaching inside his doublet, he took out the purse Lord Lumley had given him, along with the papers for Katherine.

'So, you will do it?' He enquired, adopting a brisk manner. 'You will go to my sister and tell her what to do, then travel with her and Gerard? For if you agree, you would bring them joy where there was only fear. Indeed, it could be that you will be helping to save their lives, along with your own... and in doing so, you would heal my heart.'

'By the Lord, of course I'll do it!' Hawkins said, with some warmth. 'Could you even think otherwise? I'll ride like the wind to Devon – and there will surely be joy, when I find your sister and tell her all. Will she hear more from you, in time?'

'In time, perhaps,' Revill said. 'Now you'd best take this, with my blessing.'

'Have you a message?' Hawkins enquired, as he took the purse. 'Apart from God speed to her new home?'

'Tell her I'm to be married,' Revill replied, after a moment. 'And – tell her to make me an uncle. Beyond that...' he shrugged.

Whereupon, after the other had taken Lord Lumley's papers and stowed them away, it was done. And at the last, after Revill had given his directions, their leave-taking was somewhat hurried: a firm clasp of hands, some muttered words of gratitude from Hawkins, before they both rode out of the trees down to the road. Then with a final nod the two ex-soldiers parted, Revill sitting his horse while the other urged his to a trot and finally a gallop, to disappear in the morning haze.

Revill gave a sigh, leaned down to pat Malachi's neck – then sat up with a jolt.

He had been about to turn round and ride east, back towards West Sussex. And yet, there was time for one more thing, he realised: after their last meeting, he knew Jenna would wait for his return. The distance to Portsmouth, he reckoned, was but a dozen miles, at the most fifteen: half a day's ride in summer, on a mount like Malachi. The Royal Progress would take far longer, of course, probably stopping for the night en route. There was ample time for Revill to get there, and seek out his oldest and most loyal friend – perhaps for the last time.

His one-time corporal of gunnery, Tom Bright.

A RELUCTANT HERO

SIXTEEN

It was late afternoon before he reached the old harbour town, with Southsea Castle louring down from the hill above. Sweaty and saddle-sore, and with a powerful thirst, he walked Malachi through the cobbled streets, seeking a suitable inn. Finding one that looked welcoming enough, he passed through an arch into the stable yard, dismounted and looked round for the ostler. When someone appeared, a middle-aged man, he handed over a coin and gave instructions for his horse to be fed and well-watered. That done, he was about to move off, whereupon he stopped.

'Do you know the names of the inns where seamen congregate?' He enquired.

For answer, the man put on a puzzled look. 'Do you jest, sir? There isn't an inn in this town where they don't!'

'No?' Revill looked him up and down. 'There must be one, surely. They're a superstitious lot, are they not? Somewhere they choose not to gather, for some reason or other? Call it my fancy,' he added.

'Well now...' At that, the ostler frowned. 'It strikes me you must know of it already, to ask such a question. Is it the Amity Tavern you seek?'

'Now that I think on it, perhaps it is. Can you direct me?'

'With ease, sir,' the man nodded. 'But see now, it's a low place... I might even say, a haunt of coggers and thieves. Not fit for a gentleman like yourself.'

'It sounds perfect,' Revill said. 'If you'd be so kind?'

It was a short distance to walk, to a lane off Penny Street. Leaving Malachi to be cared for at the larger inn where he had alighted, he turned down an alley and found the Amity Tavern: a squat building, with several idlers lounging outside. It was just a notion - but he knew Tom Bright, as he knew this was the kind of place he might be found. Tom loathed the sea, as he loathed sailors. Moreover, if the words of the scrawled note he had left in his lodgings were to be believed, he was a fugitive too.

Revill's chief concern was that he had taken ship and left England already. Hence, once again he would have to trust his luck: after all he was Lucky Captain Revill, who had escaped death more times than seemed possible, some men said. He could almost hear Tom mutter the words, as he stood beside a cannon on some field of combat. Brushing past the loafers, with a hand straying to his sword-hilt by instinct, Revill shoved the door open and stepped into a gloomy interior, where the smell of stale beer almost made him gag.

A few men stood about, eying him with suspicion. There was only one table, the stools all taken. Scanning the room, Revill's eyes fell on a drawer in a dirty apron, working the spigot. But when he made his way towards him, the man tensed.

'Can I aid you, master?' His gaze took in Revill's clothes and his sword, before he glanced up again with a wary look.

'Looking for a friend,' Revill said. 'Wiry little fellow, old soldier named Bright. Has he been here of late?'

His answer, however, was a shake of the head. 'I don't know names. Will you take a mug? You look like a thirsty man.'

Revill eyed him, fighting disappointment. He was weary, and felt foolish; had his journey been ill-advised? Likely Tom was long gone - and in any case, he should probably have returned to Jenna at once. With a shake of his head, he turned from the drawer and was about to take his leave, when he noticed a man at the table, on his feet and peering in his direction... then came a shout, the crash of a stool being knocked over, and a figure hurrying towards him... and at last a delighted cry, as the familiar face came into view.

'Fuck me, Captain!' Tom Bright yelled, spreading his arms. 'A miracle!'

***

It was no miracle, but it was a very powerful stroke of luck.

Having told his tale, or those parts of it he was willing to recall, Revill sat beside his old corporal, and for the first time in what seemed like an age, relaxed. They were on the rocky shorefront by the Round Tower, looking out to sea, with a jug of strong ale for company.

'So, who are they – these old foes who caught up with you in London?' He enquired, having reminded Bright of the note pinned to a bed covering in Dowgate, 'Who made you too scared even to seek a ship from Deptford? It's not like you, Tom. In truth, I never knew you to fly from any man.'

'Ah, well…' Bright paused, drank from his mug, then put on a rueful look. 'They aren't exactly old foes, in that way… not soldiers or anything. They have more of a personal score to settle, you might say. There's no reasoning with men like that, Captain. Best tie up your tail and run, I say.'

'I'm intrigued,' Revill said. 'Not Frenchmen, are they? Come to pay you out for what you did over there?'

'Not Frenchmen.' On a sudden, the little corporal looked ashamed. 'If you must draw it out of me, they're husbands. Three of them, joined forces to hunt me down on account of what they say I did with their wives.' He drank again, and met Revill's eye. 'Like I said, there's no reasoning with such.'

For a moment, Revill stared dumbly at him. Feelings rose: disbelief, then realisation – and finally something close to outrage, at his having come all this way with some vague notion of saving Tom Bright's life. And all along…

To his surprise, something unbidden surged up. His chest heaved, his mouth opened and out came a sound he had not made in a long time: a roar of uninhibited laughter. Dropping his mug, he stumbled to his feet, guffawing like a stage fool, and prompting the heads of passers-by to turn. Then he was bent double, spluttering, spittle flying. Finally, after Bright too had stood up and was looking around in embarrassment, he mastered himself and stood blinking away tears of mirth. Then he sat down heavily, and picked up his mug.

'So, I see you've managed to evade them thus far – these three husbands,' he said, recovering his breath. 'But for how much longer? Do you think they followed you here?'

'In truth, I know not, Captain,' Tom said, somewhat shamefaced. He too sat down again, and took up his own mug.

'But it don't matter now. I've got a ship… sailing in the morning for Dieppe, on the tide.' He shook his head. 'I didn't think to see you again… another day, and you'd have missed me. And I feel like a dolt, leaving that note. You've passed through Hades since then, and yet…'

He broke off, his eyes on the ground. 'Yet, you came to find me. No other man would have done that. I don't deserve a captain like you… I never did. I'm a knave, fit for naught but soldiering. So that's where I'm going: back to France. At least I can do something there… and no angry cove whose wife I might – just might – have bedded is going to follow me. It's… well, it's not like it used to be, but it'll serve.'

Finding nothing to say, Revill gazed out at the English Channel, blue and sparkling in the sunshine, and let out a sigh. Now, it seemed as if the last shred of the troubles that had weighed him down these past two years were floating away… into the air, and out to sea.

He was free at last: of the past, and free now to bid farewell to the man who had stuck with him through every hardship; the man he probably cared about more than any other. In the morning, he would see Tom off to France. Then he would return to the inn, take Malachi from the stable and ride.

Tomorrow, Queen Elizabeth's Progress of the summer of 1591 would arrive in Portsmouth, before travelling on to Southampton and then turning northwards at last, to make its laborious way back to London. But Revill would already be gone, riding by another route into West Sussex: to Burwood's farm, and at last to Jenna.

And after that, he was resolved that they would never part again.

'Well then,' he said finally, turning to his companion and clapping him on the shoulder. 'Shall we take a tour of the harbour, and you can show me the ship you're boarding? Then we might have supper, and tomorrow we'll say our farewells.'

'You don't want to come with me, then?' The little corporal enquired, with a straight face. 'No, I thought not.'

They stood up together, and began to walk.

A RELUCTANT HERO

AFTERWORD

Queen Elizabeth the First died in her seventieth year in March 1603, having indicated that her successor should be her distant cousin, King James the Sixth of Scotland. She was the last Tudor monarch.

Sir Robert Cecil rose to become the most powerful statesman in England, first Earl of Salisbury, Lord Treasurer, Secretary of State to Queen Elizabeth and then to King James, dying exhausted at the age of forty-nine in 1612.

Sir Thomas Heneage died aged sixty-three in 1595, suffering from gout, mired in debt and quarrelling with his daughter, yet still seeking political advancement to the end.

Lord John Lumley, a keen collector of art and books, died peacefully in 1609 aged seventy-six. His extensive collection, which he had willed to the Crown, would eventually form the basis of the British Library.

Captain Will Revill seems to disappear from the historical record, and is believed to have ended his days farming in his native Devonshire. It is said that his widow Jenna survived him, along with their many children.

Printed in Great Britain
by Amazon